A WOMAN TO DIE FOR

When hard-nosed P.I. Mitch Holliday
loses his licence, he helps his partner,
Lionel Banks, to pick up a missing girl
named Lila Hendricks. But everything
goes wrong; Mitch is drawn into a world
of money, murder and double-cross.
Seduced by socialite Claire Dixon's
wealth — murder is now the name of
the game. The target is a wealthy busi-
nessman with few redeeming qualities.
Would Mitch, tough and cynical as he
is, kill for the promise of love and
money?

STEVE HAYES

A WOMAN
TO DIE FOR

Complete and Unabridged

LINFORD
Leicester

First published in Great Britain

First Linford Edition
published 2011

British Library CIP Data

Hayes, Steve.
   A woman to die for. - -
   (Linford mystery library)
   1. Private investigators- -Fiction. 2. Socialites
   - -Fiction. 3. Businessmen- -Crimes against- -
   Fiction. 4. Suspense fiction.
   5. Large type books.
   I. Title II. Series
   823.9′2–dc22

   ISBN 978–1–44480–534–5

Published by
F. A. Thorpe (Publishing)
Anstey, Leicestershire

Set by Words & Graphics Ltd.
Anstey, Leicestershire
Printed and bound in Great Britain by
T. J. International Ltd., Padstow, Cornwall

To Cora with Love

Prologue

The Blue Oasis was something of a landmark on Ventura Boulevard, occupying a whole corner a few blocks west of Laurel Canyon. Opened in the sixties, it was typical of the San Fernando Valley-style motels of that era: a two-story, U-shaped building built around a parking lot. Its only distinguishing feature was a row of fake palm trees and a tacky wooden cut-out of a camel standing outside the office.

Mitchell 'Mitch' Holliday left his Ford Taurus in an alley behind the motel and sneaked around the end building, looking for room 109. He found it without much trouble, got out his camera and silently approached the door. The louvered blind was down, hiding what was happening inside the dark room, but Mitch could hear enough panting and moaning to know he had struck pay dirt.

Steadying himself, he kicked the door

in and quickly took a picture. The flash lit up the darkness, illuminating a fleshy, balding, middle-aged man and a pretty but hard-looking young blonde passionately coupled on the bed.

Shocked gasps and profanity chased Mitch from the room. Knowing that he had probably just cost local hotshot developer, Crosby Heiss, a million additional bucks' worth of alimony, Mitch hurried back to the alley to call his client, Mrs. Elyse Heiss.

As he approached his car a shadowy figure rose up behind it. For a moment Mitch thought it was one of the many homeless men and women haunting the streets and alleys of North Hollywood; but as he continued walking, he recognized the man's jowly face and dark curly hair and glimpsed the gun aimed at him.

Hurling himself sideways, he heard the loud boom of the shot followed by the whine of the bullet ricocheting off the front fender near his head.

He hit the ground, rolling over and drawing his snub-nosed .38 in the same motion, and looked up just in time to see

2

the man closing in on him between the side of his car and the rear wall of the motel.

Mitch swung his gun up and fired twice at his attacker. A large, bulky man in dark-blue sweats, he grunted painfully and collapsed in a heap. Jumping up, Mitch carefully approached the body, ready to fire again if it moved.

It didn't. Mitch checked the neck pulse to make sure the man was dead. Then holstering his gun, he unhooked his cell-phone from his belt and punched in 911.

Well, Holliday, he told himself. Now you've done it. You have finally done it. You've killed a goddamn cop.

Let's see if you can talk yourself out of this one.

1

The rabbit carcass lay, crushed, in the middle of the highway. It had been run over by a big rig and blood-caked tufts of fur were scattered about the blacktop. But Mother Nature, a tidy mistress, had seen to it the rabbit hadn't died in vain. A bunch of hungry crows squabbled among themselves for the mangled, bloody tidbits.

Across the highway stood Jake's gas station. It was a small, dingy eyesore consisting of an office, service bay, and the kind of restroom no one wants to use. An old Pontiac sedan, its brown-vinyl top cracked and peeling, was parked at the pumps. A pimply faced attendant in greasy overalls stood filling the tank. This was his first customer in hours and though he pretended to be concentrating on his job, he was actually trying to relieve his boredom by listening to what the black dude was saying on the nearby payphone. But the wind off the snow-capped High Sierras — a cold wind that chilled his cheeks and whipped his straggly hair about before blowing across the desert — hid most of the conversation.

Lionel Banks, unaware of the attendant's eavesdropping, kept his voice low out of force of habit. He was a naturally cautious man who seldom spoke above a whisper; now as he talked, chewing absently on a granola Health Bar, he kept watching the restroom door as if expecting someone to emerge, ready to hang up the moment they did.

' . . . We should hit Lake Tahoe in about an hour . . . No. Why would he be suspicious? He got no idea I'm settin' him up. We partners and partners in his eyes don't knife each other in the back. Mitch trusts me. If he didn't, I could never pull this off . . . Yeah. All you gotta do is sit tight till I pick up Lila. Then we're home free . . . Right . . . You got it. And remember, I want my green tonight. Every last dime! You start stallin', or try to skim my cut, the deal's off.'

Lionel hung up. He was a tall, muscular, moody man of forty-two with a glistening shaved head, intelligent face and hard eyes that looked at the world with perpetual angry distrust. Being a black man growing up on the squalid streets of south central Los Angeles had done that. And the fact that his old man had been a mean-assed drunk and his mother a round-heels junkie had not helped. But, what the hell, Lionel Banks wasn't making any excuses or asking for any handouts. He had failed as a professional boxer, had too much pent-up anger to pass the Los Angeles Police Department's psychiatric evaluation exam, and considered working as a city trash collector beneath him; but he'd made it to adulthood, which was more than most of his gang-banger homeys could say. And though times had been tough, he had eked out a living as a chauffeur, moon-lighted as a bounty hunter, and was now on the verge of a big score; so big, retire-ment on Easy Street lay only a few hours away.

Finishing the Health Bar, he crumpled

up the wrapper and did his Kobe Bryant nothing-but-the-bottom-of-the-net jump shot. The wrapper plunked into an empty oil drum. He then walked to his car where the attendant, the tank now full, returned the nozzle to the pump and stuck out his hand.

'Forty-nine-eighty-six, sir.'

'Hey, man, I don't want to buy the place.'

'Sorry, mister. But stuck up here in the high desert we gotta pay more for gas ourselves.'

Grudgingly, Lionel dug out fifty bucks from his jeans and handed it to the attendant. As he did, his gold-and-purple L.A. Lakers' windbreaker opened enough for the attendant to glimpse a shoulder holster with a 9mm automatic tucked snugly in it.

'Hey, slick,' Lionel said as the attendant headed for the office. 'Forget about the change and do my windshield.'

The attendant wanted to tell this city nigger where to shove his fourteen cents, but he decided not to mess with a man carrying a gun. Taking a squeegee from a bucket of dirty water, he started cleaning the windshield.

★ ★ ★

In the gas station men's room, graffiti covered the walls of the only toilet stall: crude drawings of stick figures copulating in every position imaginable, enormous breasts, and enough obscenities to fill a Tijuana bible.

Mitch Holliday eyed them curiously as he sat on the toilet, wondering what kind of mentality a person had who amused themselves with this kind of perverse pornography. But, then, he had never found pornography stimulating. It was like a nude woman. Once you had seen everything there was, nothing was left for the imagination; and to Mitch the woman hadn't been born who could live up to his imagination. But cover that same naked woman with a man's shirt that was tantalizingly long enough to hide her sweet spot — and bingo! Mitch's imagination went into overdrive. Lately, he had been working with Lionel on too many cases to be with any naked women, with or without shirts. But once this job was over, he promised himself that he was going to rectify the problem . . .

Outside, a horn honked twice. Lionel was getting impatient. Mitch reached for the toilet paper. The roll was empty. So was the paper towel rack above it. He rolled his eyes.

'Wonderful.'

2

The attendant had cleaned the windshield and was now walking around the car checking the tires. When he was finished, he told Lionel that the left front tire was almost bald. 'Want me to throw on the spare, mister?'

'That *is* the spare.'

The attendant shrugged and returned to his office. He had done his job. His conscience was clear. Now these two big-city hotshots could die, for all he cared.

Lionel checked his watch and impatiently drummed his fingers on the steering wheel. He tried to ignore the guilt gnawing in his gut, reassuring himself that Mitch deserved to be punished. But that excuse didn't fly and Lionel knew it. What Mitch had done to him, wrong as it was, didn't justify all the trouble Lionel had planned for him. And as he sat there, wrestling with his conscience, he had to remind himself not to sweat it: sure, he had sold out his integrity, and his partner, but the big payoff he was getting tonight would more than compensate for the pinch of guilt he would have to chew on for the rest of his life.

Shortly, Mitch emerged from the restroom. At forty, he was a big, powerful, low-key man with dark unruly hair, tough battered features and world-weary eyes. Body by Hummer, face by hard knocks. He wore an old windbreaker and his polo shirt, and the Rockports had seen better days. He was light-footed for his size and had an easy confident walk that strangers often mistook for a swagger. They were wrong. Mitch didn't have an ounce of swagger in him. And the only thing he was afraid of was being accused of showing off.

On reaching the pump island, he grabbed a paper towel and dried his hands before climbing into the car.

Lionel stared straight ahead, feeling less guilty when he didn't look at Mitch, and started the engine. The Pontiac lurched as its transmission slipped, then, smoke blowing from the exhaust, slowly picked up speed and they drove off.

They headed north along Highway 395. A sign pointing in the opposite direction indicated Mammoth Mountain Lakes was nine miles. Lake Tahoe and Reno lay ahead. The Pontiac climbed steadily up a ribbon of blacktop that curved between towering snowy mountains and pine forests that grew out of scrubland blackened by lava rock. Muddy clouds hung ominously over the bleak landscape.

This was God's country and Mitch, a city boy, had mixed emotions about it. He was awed by its beauty but at the same time felt humbled and stranded, like an ant on an ice floe, and was anxious to get back to his concrete jungle.

'Got my candy?'

'On the back seat.'

Mitch reached back and grabbed a box of Health Bars.

'What's this crap?'

'Fasten your seat belt, bro'.'

'I told you to buy me Snickers.'

'Granola's better for you. Now buckle up.'

'I don't want somethin' that's better for me. I want crunchy peanuts mixed in rich chewy chocolate. I hate this healthy shit. Tastes like sawdust.'

''Case you forgotten it's against the law drivin' without no seatbelt. If the CHP stops us, I'll get me a ticket.'

'Lionel — '

'No, man, I mean it. I don't got no fuckin' money to waste on goddamn tickets — '

'LIONEL — '

'What?'

'Shut the fuck up and drive.' Mitch dug out a crumpled pack of non-filtered Camels. Lighting up, he inhaled with deep satisfaction.

'Crack the window,' Lionel told him.

'You kiddin'? It's freezing butt out there.'

'Then, ditch the cancer stick. I got enough problems without dyin' from second-hand smoke.'

Mitch took a long drag, savoring every moment of it. Then he lowered the window and flipped the butt out. He exhaled a stream of smoke after it, rolled up the window and shook his head in mock disgust at Lionel.

'Know what your trouble is, partner?'

'I'm sure you gonna tell me.'

'You so worried about dyin', you ain't enjoying livin'.'

'Oh, I'm enjoyin' it, all right,' Lionel said bitterly. 'Hell, I'm havin' such a good time blowin' all my millions on coke, whores, and Cadillacs it scares the crap outta me. I mean, how'd this dumb nigger get to be so lucky?'

Mitch chuckled. 'Did you pay off Richie's braces yet?'

'With what? Every buck I make goes out faster than it comes in. You forget, man. I don't live alone, like you. I'm married. Got me responsibilities — a house, kids, and a wife spends money like water.'

'Donna? Get out. She scrapes the most out of every dime you give her.'

'Tell you that herself, did she?'

'Didn't have to. I see her every day with my own eyes, goin' back and forth to work, always in the same clothes — '

'Hey, man, don't lay no Cinderella guilt trip on me. I keep tellin' Donna to buy new outfits, but she never does. She too busy buyin' stuff for the kids.'

'Well, ain't she the selfish bitch.'

'Fuck you, man. You don't know how it is with kids. Always somethin'. Dentist, pediatrician, books for school — god-damn bills never end.'

'You feel that way, why'd you have 'em?'

Lionel ignored the question and stuck out his hand. 'Let me see Lila's picture again.'

'I don't have it.'

'Yeah, you do. I give it to you when we left L.A.'

'I know. But there wasn't any toilet paper, so — '

'Whoa. Wait a minute. Let me get this straight. You used the only photo we got of Lila Hendricks to wipe your honky ass?'

'What was I supposed to use — my shirt?'

Lionel punched the steering wheel. 'I

don't believe you, man. How we supposed to find Lila, we got no photo?'

'No sweat.' Mitch tapped his forehead. 'I got her face burned in up here. So quit worryin', okay, and concentrate on your driving. I don't want to end up road kill like that goddamn rabbit back there.'

3

They drove for several miles in tight-lipped silence, the wind off the mountains pushing against the driver's side of the car and whipping tumbleweeds across the highway in front of them. Then Mitch, tired of looking at Lionel's angry scowl, asked him what was wrong.

'Nothin'.'

'Then why you been in a foul mood since we left L.A?'

'I ain't been in no foul mood.'

'Yeah, you have. I mean, you're a gloomy bastard best of times, but today, Christ, you been acting like a dog caught his nuts on a fence.'

Lionel didn't answer. But rage boiled out of every pore on his face.

'If I've done somethin' to piss you off, man, tell me — ' Mitch broke off as suddenly the bald left front tire blew out.

Lionel fought the wheel, trying to keep the car straight, but it seemed to have a mind of its own. It swerved across the highway, careening off the shoulder and down a steep embankment. Gaining speed, it landed at the bottom so hard the passenger-side door burst open and Mitch was thrown out. He landed on his back, bounced, and rolled into some bushes. Dazed but unhurt, he raised his head and saw the car plunge into the underbrush then flip over and slide along on its roof until it crashed into a pile of rocks.

Mitch jumped up and ran to the overturned Pontiac. All four wheels were spinning slowly, like a dying bug feebly waving its antennae. Mitch hunkered down by the driver's side door. The window was broken and inside Lionel was pinned upside down between the wheel and the caved-in roof. Despite his seatbelt, he was busted up internally and every breath was agony.

Mitch pulled on the buckled door, but it had been crunched so badly it wouldn't open. He reached in through the shattered window and tried to unfasten the seatbelt. His fumbling made Lionel gasp in pain.

'No use, man. I'm toast.'

'Take it easy. You ain't gonna die.'

'Got that straight from the Man upstairs, did you?'

'I'll flag someone down. Have 'em take me to a phone so I can call a hospital.'

'No, don't go, man.' Lionel, who had never known fear before, became panicky. 'Try your cell again. M-Maybe we close enough now to Tahoe to pick up a signal.'

Mitch obeyed. But his cell-phone wouldn't respond. 'It's no use. I gotta go get help.'

'No! Stay with me, bro'. I'm scared.'

Mitch, without thinking, dug out a cigarette, lit it and put it between Lionel's bloodied lips.

Lionel angrily spat it out and coughed up blood. 'What's the matter? Ain't I dyin' fast enough for you?'

The two men looked at each other. Both knew it was hopeless and both knew they knew. But they also knew dying was something you did alone and neither man could think of what to say to make it easier. Finally, Lionel said:

'Why me, bro'? I got a family. I pump

iron every day. Don't do no drugs. Even use my seatbelt. Why the hell me?'

'If I knew the answer to that, pal, I'd be on *Jeopardy*.'

'That's it? That's your goddamn pearl of wisdom? I'm puking blood and you talkin' fuckin' game shows?'

'Hey, don't bust my balls,' Mitch said. 'What d'you want from me? Life sucks.'

'Some comfort you are . . . ' Lionel coughed up more blood. 'What's next, one of your stupid Ali Baba parables?'

Mitch ignored Lionel's sarcasm. 'Don't move until I get back, okay?' He started to walk away but Lionel fumbled out his gun and aimed it at Mitch.

'You ain't goin' nowhere.'

Mitch froze.

'You so goddamn smart, think you got all the answers, tell me why I'm dyin' and you ain't.' He shoved the 9mm into Mitch's face, adding: ''Cause we both know you the one deserve to die.'

Mitch sagged like he had been sucker-punched. 'I wondered when you'd get around to dropping that on me.'

'Just waitin' for the right moment.'

'*This* is the right moment?'

'What, you think I planned on dyin'?'

Mitch guiltily avoided Lionel's glare. 'How long you known about Donna and me?'

'Almost from the gitgo.'

'Why didn't you say something?'

''Cause I wanted you to suffer, man, same as I did every time I thought about you stickin' it to my old lady.'

'Well, you got your wish. I've felt like shit ever since.'

'Some consolation that is.'

'So, what happens next? You gonna shoot me or do I go for help?'

Lionel didn't answer. He drifted off somewhere, his eyes rolling up into his head until all Mitch could see were the blood-rimmed whites. Then recovering, he said weakly: 'Th-that story you told me — one about dyin' before you're supposed to — tell me it again.'

'Lionel, for Chrissake — '

'I mean it, sucker.' Lionel pressed the gun against Mitch's sweaty forehead. 'Give me a 'Once upon a time' or I swear I'll make it a double funeral — ' He broke off, coughing blood everywhere.

Mitch, sensing Lionel was about to shoot him, decided to stall the inevitable. 'Once upon a time,' he said grimly, 'there was this servant in Baghdad, see, who comes runnin' into the palace and tells his master he saw Death hanging out in the marketplace. He's scared out of his mind and his master says, okay, okay, be cool. I'll handle it. He gives his servant a horse so the guy can ride to Samarra and hide out, then goes to the marketplace and asks Death why the hell she frightened his servant — '

'Whoa. D-Death's a chick?'

'Sure.'

'What about that old dude you see in pictures, one with a long beard holdin' a weed-whacker?'

'That's Old Testament crap. Like thinking the world's flat. Death's really a hot young babe with a voice like melted cheese.'

Lionel grinned weakly. 'G-Go on, bro'.'

' 'I'm sorry,' Death says to the master. 'I didn't mean to scare your servant. I was just surprised to see him there.' 'Why's that,' the master asks. 'Because,' Death says, 'I have an appointment with him later in Samarra.''

Lionel wasn't listening. Blood dribbled from his mouth as he whispered: 'Mitch, I . . . I'm sorry, man.'

'Forget it.'

'G-Go home, bro'. This gig ain't for real. I b-been lyin' to you . . . all along.'

'What're you talkin' about?'

'Don't g-go to Harrah's, man. It's a set up. That bitch Lila's w-waitin' for . . . '

'For what?'

'Look in the book, bro' . . . F-Find the key . . . '

'What key? Lionel, what're you tryin' to tell me?'

'Like in the s-story . . . Samarra . . . Not knowin' you in the wrong place, wrong time. You go to Harrah's, man, and you a dead cigar. Here . . . ' Lionel dug something small out of his pocket and handed it to Mitch. 'Take this. It'll clue you in. And d-don't forget your p-promise to me . . . '

Lionel died with his eyes staring emptily ahead.

Mitch sighed. He had not known Lionel very long, but during the time they had been partners he had grown to like the man. But one of Mitch's assets was his ability to shut out problems, to adjust quickly, no matter how bad the situation; and after a moment of remorse, he cut off his emotions, reached in through the broken window, and gently closed Lionel's eyelids.

'You're right,' he told the corpse. 'It *is* a lousy deal. Should've been me, not you.' Wondering how he was going to break the news to Donna and the kids, Mitch grabbed the keys from the ignition, stood up, and looked at the object in his hand. It was a piece from a jigsaw puzzle. The front was red as a desert sunset; on the back was written: I LOVE YOU.

Wondering what it meant, Mitch tucked the piece of jigsaw puzzle in his wallet. Long ago he had discovered that mysteries, like life, had a strange way of resolving themselves. All you had to do was be patient; to wait for the unraveling to stop and then draw your own conclusions.

He walked to the rear of the car. Gasoline dripped from the ruptured gas tank. Mitch opened the upside down trunk. Out fell two overnight bags, one his and the other Lionel's, a tire iron, jack, some oily rags, a shotgun, .38 snub-nosed revolver, 9mm automatic, and two boxes of shells. Mitch frowned, surprised. He knew Lionel usually kept his guns locked in his bedroom closet. Why now had he decided to put them in the trunk? And when did he do it? Certainly not in the last few days, because they'd been together in San Diego rounding up a bail-skipper, coming home late last night, so whacked out they'd gone straight to bed; and certainly not this morning, while they were getting ready to leave for Lake Tahoe, because Mitch had been in the house, drinking coffee with Lionel's wife, Donna, when Lionel had come from the bedroom carrying only his overnight bag.

So, when? Another mystery! Mitch shrugged it off and stuffed the handguns and the ammo into his overnight bag. Next he broke down the shotgun and tucked the two pieces into the bag as well. The movement caused his jacket to flap open, revealing a shoulder holster holding a .45 automatic.

Leaving Lionel's bag where it fell, he picked up his own bag and walked a short distance away. There he stopped, lit up a Camel, deliberately flipped the cigarette at the rear of the Pontiac, and ran toward the highway.

The cigarette fell into a pool of gasoline. Flames burst up. They spread to the car and ignited the ruptured gas tank. There was a loud fiery explosion. The blast pushed against Mitch's back as flaming debris sailed everywhere. He waited until he reached the highway before looking back at the burning wreck. By his expression it was hard to know what he was thinking, but it wasn't pretty.

'Rest easy, partner,' he said softly. He then turned and continued on along the highway in the direction of Lake Tahoe.

4

Harrah's was downtown on the Nevada side of the border overlooking the calm, silvery lake. Mitch parked the Dodge compact he had rented from Avis in the parking lot, and entered the plush hotel. Compared to outside, it was like stepping into a sauna. He unzipped his windbreaker and took stock of things. The lobby was full of skiers; healthy, athletic men and women with sun- and windburned faces dressed in colorful sweaters and tight-fitting stretch pants that showed off their hard, perky buns. Mitch, a legs and rear-end man, took an appreciative look around then entered the casino.

The large brightly lit room was packed with losers and dreamers trying to beat the house. The grinding, rhythmic roar of slot machines filled Mitch's ears — levers being pulled, coins dropping into slots, the clattering metallic jingle as jackpots were hit and coins cascaded into metal trays.

Mitch made his way between the rows of one-armed bandits, his eyes taking in everything around him as he looked for Lila Hendricks. He came to the end of the aisle, turned, and started up another. He did this three more times and still saw no sign of Lila.

He paused. His shoes were scuffed and dirty and his feet hurt from all the walking he'd done before a cowboy in an old pickup gave him a ride. The cowboy, a bull-rider on his way to a rodeo in Reno, chewed Redman tobacco and spat into an empty lid wedged into the console cup holder. He apologized every time he spat, even after Mitch said it was okay; said his name was Wiley but that everyone called him Amarillo (after a bull that stomped his daddy, not the city) and how he didn't mind if Mitch smoked and even offered him 'fixin's' when Mitch ran out of Camels.

Mitch surprised himself by remembering how to roll a smoke without spilling all the loose tobacco, and by the time they pulled into Tahoe and Amarillo dropped Mitch off at an Avis rental car agency, the two had killed a pint of Jack Daniels and compared notes on everything from broken bones to country-western music and the merits of Willie Nelson vis-à-vis Garth Brooks.

Now, as Mitch started down the final aisle, he forgot about his aching dogs and thought about the cowboy and how cool it would be to have a son just like him, so they could share all the good times the world had to offer. But it wasn't in the cards. Mitch was a coward when it came to commitment. And when women started making sounds like expectant brides, he simply faded away.

He stopped and lowered his gaze. Directly ahead was a pair of stiletto-heeled pumps worn by a brassy-haired bimbo in a leather mini-skirt as red as her shoes.

Bingo, Mitch thought as he saw her face.

The girl did not notice Mitch. She was too busy popping silver dollars into the slot and pulling the lever as fast as the machine would allow. Each time the bars, bells and fruits stopped in different positions, but never a winner.

'Come on, baby . . . please . . . hit it big for momma . . .'

The girl dropped in another dollar and pulled the lever. The fruits stopped whirling in the tiny window. One cherry. Two cherries. Three cherries! Silver dollars cascaded out of the machine, overflowing the tray and spilling out onto the carpet as a five-hundred-dollar jackpot paid off!

The girl screamed excitedly and began jumping up and down. 'Yes! Yes! Yessss! I won! I finally won!'

Everyone stopped playing their machines and stared enviously at her. The girl stopped jumping around and started scooping up the silver dollars.

'Must be your lucky night, Lila.'

Lila Hendricks whirled around and saw Mitch standing before her.

'How you know my name?' she asked. 'Who are you?'

'A friend of Lionel's.'

'I don't know any Lionels.'

'He knows you. And he paid me to help him take you back to L.A.' Mitch closed in. 'Now, let's go.'

'Like hell!' Lila hurled a handful of silver dollars in Mitch's face and took off. Mitch followed. Her mini-skirt was designed for many things, but running wasn't one of them. Mitch quickly caught up and grasped her from behind. She fought him, scratching and kicking, until they both went sprawling.

Mitch pinned Lila to the floor and grabbed for his handcuffs.

'I got a thousand bucks stashed in my motel,' she hissed as he cuffed her. 'Let me go and it's yours.' Then, when he didn't answer: 'I'll let you do me, too. Seven ways to Sunday. How 'bout it?'

'Why should I trust you?'

'Lionel did.'

'I'll think it over.' Mitch dragged her up, waved off the approaching security officers and led her away.

Among the crowd of onlookers was Lila's tattooed punker boyfriend, Joey Gibson. Nose dribbling from too much coke, he gave Mitch and Lila a head start and then followed them.

Winning is all that matters in a casino. Once Mitch and Lila were gone, everyone returned to their gambling as if nothing had happened.

At a nearby blackjack table, Claire Dixon had also seen Lila's capture. By her aloof expression it was impossible to know what she was thinking. But behind dark glasses her ice-blue eyes blazed with angry frustration. Where was Lionel, she wondered. He was supposed to be here by now. How the hell could everything have gotten so messed up?

Tipping the dealer a five-dollar chip, she gave her stool to an old fat woman with nicotine-stained white hair hovering behind her.

Claire was a knockout. But it wasn't her elegant Nordic beauty or long gold hair that men found so irresistible. It was her innate vulnerability, the same combination of sexiness and helpless wide-eyed innocence that fifty years ago Norma Jeane parlayed into becoming Marilyn Monroe; an intangible quality that can't be acquired, but was worth more than diamonds and had men rushing to protect her, no matter the consequences.

Claire paused, a few steps from the blackjack table and looked around for her younger sister. Through the mass of bobbing heads she saw Elaina playing craps across the aisle.

Elaina was a willowy, beautiful redhead in her mid-twenties. At first look, she seemed almost as innocent as Claire. But a second look said that beneath her pouty desirable exterior, she was dangerously unstable. If life were fair, she would have worn a sign warning men away; but life wasn't fair and the only sign that told wise men to keep their fly closed around her was the infantile way she sucked her left thumb. She'd sucked it since birth, causing a hollow ridge in the roof of her mouth that made her speak with a provocative, sexy lisp. But that wasn't all it did; according to the legion of men she had seduced, the ridge rubbed the head of their penis in a way that gave new meaning to the word 'erotic'!

Elaina wore a clingy gold gown with a split up the side that partly hid her crippled legs. She could barely walk and supported herself with the aid of two metal sticks with elbow grips.

Claire ignored the twinge of guilt she always felt when she saw the crutches and quickly joined her sister.

'Lionel hasn't showed,' she whispered.

'Oh, shit,' Elaina said. 'You think something's gone wrong?

'I don't know yet. I'm going back to the room to see if there's any messages.'

'Want me to come with you?'

'Uh-uh. You stay here. It's all right,' Claire said as Elaina grew panicky. 'There's nothing to be afraid of.'

'Like hell there isn't!'

'Shhh. Keep your voice down.'

'That's what you said last time, remember? And look where that got us.'

'Trust me,' Claire said. 'Have I ever let you down?'

'Uh-uh.'

'Then calm down and let me work this out.' Claire kissed her sister on the cheek and hurried off.

Elaina looked around for Mace and Taggert. They stood a few steps away, ever watchful; two large brutish enforcers in dark glasses and trendy Italian suits who were ready to strong arm anyone who gave Elaina the slightest grief.

What a freaking nightmare, she thought bitterly. *And I'm trapped right smack in the middle of it!*

5

The State Line Motel was unique in the fact that the border line ran down the center of its eighteen units. It was two levels of faded brown-and-white stucco, had a swimming pool out front, and above the tacky office was a gaudy blinking neon sign with several bulbs missing. The owner didn't bother to repaint the place or fix the sign because all the rooms were always occupied. Seems the idea of men and women screwing while her breasts were in Nevada and his dick was in California was enough of a novelty to keep the motel filled forever. Below the neon sign the words 'No Vacancy' were frozen in horny perpetuity.

In Room 9 everything was dark, shadowy and seedy. Nothing romantic ever happened here. The blinking neon sign flashed through the Venetian blinds like a disco strobe light. It showed intermittent glimpses of Mitch and Lila making love on the bed. Her left wrist was cuffed to the headboard; her purse lay open on the bed. Ten crisp one-hundred-dollar bills were piled beside it.

Lila's heated moaning hid the sound of the door opening. Joey Gibson snuck in. He paused just inside the door, saw what was happening and aimed his hand-cannon at Mitch.

'Party's over, bozo!'

Mitch froze in mid-stroke, his naked body keeping Lila pinned to the bed.

Joey grinned at him. 'Should thank me, mister.'

'Yeah, why's that?'

'I'm gonna make you a highlight on the eleven o'clock news.' He imitated a television newscaster: 'Reports say the poor sucker died in the saddle.' Joey giggled inanely and started to squeeze the trigger. 'Giddyup, cowboy — '

Mitch threw himself sideways and at the same time used his left hand to jerk Lila in front of him.

Joey fired, twice, the bullets punching holes in Lila's big silicone breasts. She screamed and went limp in Mitch's grasp.

Joey stared at what he had done, momentarily stunned.

Mitch grabbed his .45 automatic from under the pillow next to him and fired. The single heavy boom of the big Colt bounced off the walls. Joey went down, a bullet in his chest, dead before he hit the floor.

Mitch turned to Lila. Blood trickled from her lipstick-smeared mouth. She was fading fast and could barely talk.

'T-Tell Lionel I'm sorry I fucked things up.'

'What things?'

Her lips moved but no words came out.

'Lila, talk to me. What were you and L.B. mixed up in?'

' . . . W-Was Joey's idea. Me'n him, we were s'posed to help Lionel waste the old man . . . '

'What old man?'

'All Joey's fault. He found out about the jewelry an' — '

'Jewelry?'

'D-Diamonds . . . the ones Joey stole from Lionel. Said we's gonna be m-m-millionaires . . . '

She died. Mitch felt her neck. No pulse.

'Damn.' Keeping an ear out for police sirens, he quickly dressed then knelt beside the dead punk and took out Joey's wallet. It was filled with tens and twenties. Without any qualms Mitch pocketed the money and looked at the California driver's license. It read 'Joey S. Gibson' and gave an address in Van Nuys, one of countless towns that made up the vast sprawling community known as the San Fernando Valley. Mitch, who lived within gunshot of Reseda, knew it well. He put the wallet back and searched the rest of Joey's pockets. Empty. Not even car keys.

Disappointed, he walked to the bed and listened. Still no sirens. Was he going to be lucky for a change; had no one heard the shots? He pocketed Lila's ten one-hundred-dollar bills, dumped out her purse and went through its contents. There was the usual female paraphernalia, plus a wallet that Mitch robbed of ninety dollars, and a driver's license listing Lila's address in North Pasadena.

Mitch stored all the info' away, returned everything to the purse, and looked under the mattress. Nothing. Next, he looked under the bed. Again, nothing! He moved to the armoire. All the drawers were empty. Jesus, didn't these kids use underwear? He opened the closet. Lila and Joey's clothes hung in it. A briefcase lay on the shelf above them. Mitch took it down, opened it, saw it too was empty and threw it down in disgust. Where the hell had they hidden the jewels, he wondered.

His gaze settled on the bed. The headboard was several inches from the wall. He had not noticed it when he'd cuffed Lila's wrist to it earlier, but then, hey, his mind had been on other things. Now, he peered behind it and saw a wooden cigar box taped to the wall.

'Hel-lo . . . ' He pulled the box loose and opened it, revealing a glittering pile of diamond jewelry: bracelets, rings, necklaces, earrings. Jesus, he thought, heart pumping. How the hell did Lionel, who had never rubbed more than a few bucks together in his whole miserable life, get involved in a major heist? And when? And who was he was mixed up with? Deciding he would worry about the answers later, Mitch stuffed the cigar box into the briefcase and left the room.

As he started toward his rental car, flashing red-and-blue lights caught his attention. Two sheriff squad cars, sirens silent, were pulling up to the manager's office. Trapped, Mitch ducked into the breezeway and hid the briefcase between the Coke machine and ice-maker that were set against the wall. He then ran back into Lila's room, dialed 'O' for office and told the operator: 'There's been a shooting. Call the cops.'

6

There were now three Sheriff's Department units parked outside Lila's room, one of them belonging to the sheriff. Whirling lights flashed. Radios crackled. Paramedics loaded two corpse-filled body bags into an ambulance.

Nearby, Mitch stood beside Sheriff Harlan Briggs, a big, flinty-eyed ramrod of a man in his late fifties who was examining Mitch's I.D. He wore a gray Stetson, brown sheepskin coat over civilian clothes, olive green pants tucked into snow-boots, and his speech and every movement he made was slow and deliberate; methodical. His face was weathered, his mustache gray and drooping, and his sun-strained blue eyes full of integrity. But the corners of his mouth were twisted with contempt, indicating he did not think much of Mitch.

'Okay, Holliday, I reckon you're who you say you are.'

'My creditors will be happy to hear that.'

Sheriff Briggs was not amused. He glared at Mitch and in a grim raspy voice, said: 'Mister, you know anything 'bout hemorrhoids?'

'They hurt.'

'Goddamn right, they hurt. An' I got 'em bad. Real bad. So don't mess with me, soldier, an' maybe, just maybe, I won't throw your sorry ass in jail.' He handed Mitch his I.D. 'What do you know about the suspects?'

'The guy I know nothin' about, 'cept he tried to shoot me. The girl, Lila Hendricks, worked as a maid for a rich family in San Marino and supposedly ripped off some credit cards.'

'And you were hired to bring her back?'

'My partner, Lionel Banks, was hired. I came along as back up.'

'Did that include screwing her brains out?'

Mitch grinned. 'Wouldn't deprive me of one of the few perks this crappy job has to offer, would you, sheriff?'

Sheriff Briggs gingerly shifted his

weight from one foot to the other, moving like a man who had barb-wire between his legs.

'Where's your partner now?'

'Good question.'

'How about a good answer?'

'He dropped me off at the casino where I grabbed Lila, and I haven't seen him since. If that's all,' Mitch added, 'I could use some shuteye.'

Sheriff Briggs eyed Mitch like he was dying to lock him up. But first he needed evidence on which to build his case.

'Go ahead,' he sighed. 'But don't leave Tahoe without telling me.'

'You got it.' Mitch turned to leave, felt a moment of compassion and looked back at the sheriff. 'Drink lots of water.'

'Say what?'

'And no starchy foods.'

'*What?*'

'Starchy foods. Stay away from 'em.'

'If you're yanking my chain, soldier — '

'No, no, this is on the up and up. Constipation is what causes hemorrhoids. You know. Strainin' too hard on the john.'

The sheriff gritted his teeth and looked

45

at Mitch as if he could not believe his goddamn gall. 'Is that so?'

'Sure. You gotta eat more fiber. Fiber's the key.'

'Any *other* helpful hints?'

'Buy a doughnut.'

'Doughnut?'

'Right. You know. A rubber cushion with a hole in the middle. Helps when you sit down.' Mitch smiled the smile of a guardian angel. 'Nighty-night, now.' He walked off.

A perky female newscaster, with a mini-cam crew, stopped Mitch as he walked up and held a mike in his face.

'Ready for our interview now, Mr. Holliday?'

'Sure thing, honey. Fire away.'

*   *   *

Mitch entered his motel room and closed the door without turning on the light. He moved to the window and peered through the louvered blinds. Outside, a sheriff squad car was parked across the street. Mitch grinned. What did Sheriff Briggs think he was . . . an amateur?

46

Stretching out on the bed he used his cell phone to call Lionel's wife, Donna, in Reseda.

'Hi, it's me.'

'Oh, hi. Where's Lionel?'

'How should I know? He's your husband.'

'Don't start with me, Mitch. I'm not in the mood.'

'What? You got a monopoly on bad moods?'

The line went dead in his ear as she banged down the phone. Mitch heaved a sigh and redialed Donna's number.

'Don't hang up,' he said quickly, adding: 'Look, I'm sorry if you're having a shitty day. Just tell me if L.B. was into any stuff that I don't know about.'

'What kind of stuff?'

'Baby, if I knew what kind of stuff, would I be askin' you? Stuff-stuff. Now, answer my question, dammit.'

'Up yours,' Donna said. 'I don't have to answer you about anything.'

'Okay, okay,' he said, 'don't go ballistic on me. I'm just trying to figure somethin' out.'

47

'Like, what?'

'Lila Hendricks. That name mean anything to you?'

'No. Why, was Lionel doing her?'

'How should I know? I'm not his keeper.'

'Then why'd you bring her up?'

'Because,' Mitch said, holding the phone away from his ear, 'I wondered if you'd ever heard Lionel mention her name. *Jesus!*'

He ended the call and went into the bathroom to brush his teeth.

7

It was five after nine the next morning when Claire crossed the glittering lobby of Harrah's to the front desk and asked the desk clerk if she had any messages. The clerk, a veteran hotel employee whose job fed him a steady diet of movie stars and supermodels, found himself trapped by her sensual beauty and little girl helplessness.

'S-Sorry, ma'am,' he said, coming out of his reverie. 'I didn't hear you.'

Claire, quietly amused by her power over men, showed no irritation as she repeated her question. The clerk dragged his eyes away from her perfectly tanned face and moist kiss-me lips and checked the computer.

'No, ma'am. Anything else I can do for you?'

'If a Mr. Lionel Banks calls, I'll be in the restaurant or the casino,' Claire said. 'Be sure to page me.'

She walked off. The desk clerk watched her go. He wanted her so bad it hurt. So did two hardened bellhops and a gray-haired concierge gathered nearby. Each one heaved a sigh of regret, knowing that this was as close to having her he was ever going to get.

★   ★   ★

Across town in the low-rent district Mitch stepped out of his motel room and deliberately paused, in full view of everyone, to fire up a Camel. Above the flame of his lighter his eyes darted about, taking in everything. The sheriff's squad car was still parked across the street. A deputy sat at the wheel, pretending to be filling out a logbook while actually watching Mitch's every move.

Mitch smiled to himself, exhaled a lungful of smoke and casually walked to his Dodge compact.

Fifteen minutes later he was in Harrah's sports bar, eating breakfast, reading the newspaper and betting on a horse named Banjo Lady at Saratoga.

A bank of TVs showed a variety of sports taped across the country. The set behind the bar was airing a news update featuring the same female newscaster interviewing Mitch outside Lila's motel room. She was playing up to the camera, trying to be very professional but too damned perky and pretty to be taken seriously; especially by Mitch, who seemed more interested in her ass than her questions. Not that it mattered. The sound was turned off so no one could hear what was being said, anyway.

Mitch watched his horse lose by six lengths. It's only money, he told himself. He looked at the front page of his newspaper. The headline story included photos of the State Line Motel, both corpses, and an unflattering mug shot of Mitch. The caption under his photo read: 'L.A. Bounty Hunter Involved in Motel Shootout.'

Wonderful, Mitch thought. Just what he needed when he was trying to stay out of trouble in hopes of getting his P.I. license reinstated. Behind him, he felt rather than saw every head at the bar turn as someone entered.

Mitch turned, expecting to see a celebrity. Instead, he saw Claire approaching in a dazzling white outfit that was made of some kind of clingy material. The sight of her hit him like a runaway truck. She seemed to permeate his entire body and, once inside, took possession of his soul. No woman had ever stirred him quite the way she did. All he could think of was wishing a lion were loose in the bar, so he could be a hero and save her from it.

No lion was available, so Mitch hoped for the next best thing: that Claire would notice him. She didn't. She waltzed past him, chin tilted upward, eyes staring straight ahead, sat at the bar and ordered a Bloody Mary.

Mitch knew he was no handsome charmer, but he also knew that if he let this goddess walk in and out of his life without trying to meet her, he'd hate himself forever. But how could he introduce himself without sounding like a lounge lizard? He mulled over a dozen different ways. All sounded like he wore a pencil-thin mustache, and he dismissed every one of them. When it came to women, he had never been good with words. What seemed cool in his mind always sounded slick and corny by the time it reached his mouth. He also knew that, although he presented an image of strength and rocklike self-confidence, at times his mind got squirrelly and made him feel inadequate.

This was one of those times and he was about to throw in the towel when he remembered what his high school prom queen told him when she was all grown up and about to get married. It was at her reception party and surprise, surprise, Missy had asked him to dance with her. As they clung to each other on the crowded dance floor, she suddenly giggled and in a voice slurred by champagne whispered in his ear: 'Why didn'tcha ever ask me out?' and he said ''Cause I didn't think you'd go,' and she said, 'Well, I would've, you know, I would've at the drop of a friggin' hat. Everybody thinks,' she went on, 'that because you're the prettiest girl in school, you get asked out all the time. Well, I'm here to tell you, you don't.'

'Get outta here,' he said and she said, 'It's the truth, honey. I can't count the number of Friday and Saturday nights I sat at home wishing I wasn't so pretty and guys didn't treat me like I was on a pedestal way out of their reach.' She was on a champagne-induced roll now and she added: 'You never knew this but I thought you were so hot and kept hoping you'd ask me out, but you never did, you putz, and serves you right, 'cause now I'm getting married and I won't be available.'

But she was, of course; less than two months later Mitch bumped into her at the Woodland Hills shopping mall and they had barely gotten over their surprise at seeing one another when she looked at him as only a woman who wants to get laid can, and he had recognized the look and without a word taken her hand and led her out to his car, where they got all steamed up in the front seat; and later, undressing each other as he drove, they had gone to a motel on Topanga Canyon Boulevard and spent the afternoon in bed.

With this rosy memory in mind, Mitch felt brave enough to hit on Claire. Leaving money on the table for his check, he joined her at the bar. She looked even more dazzling close up and smelled of wet lilacs behind her ears.

Mitch tried not to be intimidated, but the man who had no qualms about facing three armed gang-bangers in a dark alley felt his mouth go dry and his mind turn to mush. *Terrific*, he thought. *This goddess enters your life and what happens, you have a brain fade.*

'Hi,' he said casually. 'I'm Mitch Holliday. Can I buy you a drink?'

When Claire ignored him, he toyed with his room key and answered himself.

'Well, hello, Mitch, I'm fill-in-the-blanks. Nice to meet you.'

'Get a life,' she said, not looking at him.

'I'm tryin' to, but beautiful women keep blowin' me off.'

'Surprise, surprise.'

Mitch felt his chance already slipping away. 'You mean I'm not irresistible?'

Claire rolled her eyes and sighed. Finishing her drink, she tucked a five under the glass and gave him a withering look.

'Let me give you some free advice, cowboy: If you're looking to get laid, call a hooker. If you want to talk, call your bookie.'

'What if I want to get laid *and* talk?'

'Call your wife.' Claire slid down from her stool and started away.

Mitch knew he should keep his mouth shut but he could not help saying: 'What if I'm not married, just lonely?'

'Buy a puppy.' She walked off. All eyes watched her leave and then regretfully dragged themselves back to the various TVs.

So much for trying to be cool, Mitch thought. He had finally met a woman who lived up to his imagination and he could not even hold her long enough to find out her name! Disgusted with himself, he turned to the bartender who was eyeing him as if he were road kill.

'Puppies are good,' he said, trying to joke away his embarrassment. 'Ever own a puppy?'

'Never did.'

'You're lucky. My old man killed mine when I was six.'

'Do tell.'

'Came home one night, all sauced up, and caved its furry little head in with a bottle of Gallo red.'

'Sounds like you had a fun childhood, Jack.'

'Oh-yes-indeedy,' Mitch said. 'It was a laugh a minute.' He got off his stool and walked out.

8

Mitch went out through the hotel kitchen, so the deputy parked out front would not see him, and drove to the State Line Motel. There, he parked behind the pool, got out and fired up a Camel. Through his exhaled smoke he saw that no one was watching him and ducked into the breezeway. Reaching between the Coke machine and the ice-maker, he groped around for the briefcase.

Nothing. His heart sank.

'This what you're lookin' for, soldier?'

Mitch whirled around and saw Sheriff Briggs standing nearby, briefcase in his left hand. His right hand rested on his gun and there was a glint in his gunfighter eyes that warned Mitch not to mess with him.

Sheriff Briggs was a man who demanded instant respect. Mitch just stood there, like a schoolboy in trouble, as the sheriff cuffed his hands behind his back.

'Want to tell me what this is all about?'

'We're takin' a little ride, soldier.' Walking stiff-legged, wincing with each step, the sheriff led Mitch to his squad car and locked the briefcase in the trunk. He waited while Mitch got in on the passenger side, then came around and opened the driver's side door. A rubber cushion with a hole in the middle sat on the seat.

Mitch grinned. 'Glad to see you took my advice.'

Sheriff Briggs didn't answer. He eased himself carefully into the car, onto the cushion, grimacing with pain, let out a sigh, and closed the door.

'My ol' man had hemorrhoids,' Mitch said cheerfully. 'Poor bastard. Walked like he had a hot poker up his ass.'

Sheriff Briggs winced and started the engine.

'Finally got so bad, he had to have the suckers cut out. Said it hurt like a sonofabitch.'

Sheriff Briggs gave Mitch a gritted, wolfish smile. 'Thanks for sharing that with me, Holliday.'

They drove off, Mitch chuckling under his breath.

★ ★ ★

They headed south around the lake, hooked up with 395 and didn't stop until they reached the long black skid marks that indicated where Lionel's Pontiac had careened off the highway. Parking on the shoulder behind two CHP units, Sheriff Briggs led Mitch down the embankment and across the desert to the wreck.

It was cold and wintry. The wind off the mountains stung Mitch's cheeks and whipped up the sandy dirt. Tumbleweeds rolled past them, bouncing happily along until they got trapped against an old white tow-truck. The truck had 'Jake's Garage' painted on its doors and was parked behind the charred wreckage of what had once been Lionel's Pontiac. The driver, the young grease monkey who had pumped Lionel's gas, sat in the cab, drinking hot coffee and listening to the radio crackling out service calls.

Sheriff Briggs, with Mitch in tow, joined

two CHP Officers in mirrored sunglasses who were examining the wreck.

'Any sign yet of another corpse?'

The taller of the two CHP Officers shook his head. 'Uh-uh. All we got so far is a 9mm and what's left of the driver.' He referred to his notepad, holding the wind-fluttered page down with his thumb, and nodded toward the tow-truck. 'Kenny, there, says there were definitely two dudes in the car when it drove out. One black, one white. The white guy fits his description,' thumbing at Mitch.

'Figures.' Sheriff Briggs shifted uncomfortably on his feet, the pain almost bringing tears to his eyes. 'I'll take it from here, fellas. Thanks for responding to my call, huh?'

'Any time, Sheriff.' The Officers returned to their cars.

Sheriff Briggs gave Mitch a sour look. 'Why'd you lie to me, soldier?'

'Figured I was in enough trouble without tryin' to explain a dead partner.'

''Specially if you're trying to hide something.'

'Like, what? It was an accident, Sheriff. A tire blew out.'

'I called LAPD.'

Mitch felt an invisible punch to his stomach. 'So, now you know I was once a P.I.'

'Who got busted for money laundering.'

'I was framed. But I guess the bastards forgot to mention that.'

'What about the briefcase?'

'It's not mine. I found it in Lila's motel room after the shooting.'

'And the jewels inside it?'

'They're not mine, either.'

'And I just bet you were gonna turn everything in, right?'

'I'm not sure *what* I was gonna do.'

'That's why you stashed everything beside the Coke machine — to give yourself time to decide what you were going to do?'

'I hid the stuff there 'cause I knew nobody'd believe I wasn't involved. I also hid it 'cause I needed time to figure out how my partner was involved.'

'Maybe I can help you there.'

'Save your breath. I know what you're thinkin'. You're thinkin' me and Lionel came up here lookin' for a fence. You're thinkin' Lila and Joey were in on the deal. And when they thought I'd wasted Lionel, they wanted a bigger cut, so I blew them away, too.'

'Son, you're reading my mind.'

'It's not hard.' Mitch nodded back at his handcuffs. 'Lucky you cuffed me when you did. Trigger-happy thief like me, hey, no telling how many more folks I might've gunned down.'

Sheriff Briggs studied Mitch like a wolf hungering for an elk. Then he released his frustration in a long, weary sigh. He dug out a key, wincing at every movement, and unlocked the handcuffs.

Mitch deadpanned: 'What, you ain't arresting me?'

'You know that expression: give a guy enough rope . . . ?'

'Yeah, but hanging's not on my menu.'

'We'll see.'

'Don't hold your breath.'

'I'm not aiming to,' Sheriff Briggs said. Then, as it hit him: 'Oh, and don't tell anybody Lionel's kicked the bucket.'

'Why not?'

'I want to do some nosing around 'fore the media turns this into a goddamn circus.'

'And of course you'll tell me what you find?'

'Save your sarcasm for someone whose ass isn't on fire.' The sheriff shifted positions painfully. 'One thing I *can* tell you — something you might find interesting — all that jewelry in the cigar box; it was paste.'

Mitch's mouth dropped.

'Hit me the same way,' Sheriff Briggs said. 'Doesn't make a lick of sense, does it?' He turned and limped back toward the highway, leaving Mitch staring after him.

9

Fate, Mitch realized long ago, had no conscience. It was not driven by vengeance or compassion, malice or remorse, justice or injustice. It merely existed, for reasons beyond human understanding, randomly striking at anyone, and always when a person least expected it. Everyone was its target; its victim. No one could escape it or alter its inexorable course. Try to run away and you ran right into it. Reverse directions and there it was, waiting for you. That's what made it so frightening; so perfect.

Fate could not be manipulated.

Mitch thought about this as he sat on the hood of his rented Dodge compact in the parking lot of a Chinese takeout restaurant, finishing a carton of rice, vegetables, and teriyaki chicken. Mitch knew all about Fate. Hell, he had spent a lifetime sparring with it. Always respecting it; always treating it with kid gloves;

never complaining when it dealt him a blow or gloating when it didn't. Knowing all along that he couldn't dodge it but at the same time hoping that if he didn't thumb his nose at it, he might just squeak through life without Fate ever dealing him a fatal blow — like it had Lionel.

Lionel, Lionel, Lionel, Mitch thought as he picked a grain of rice from between his teeth with a chopstick. Man, what the hell were you mixed up in? And what were you trying to tell me when you croaked? Well, no hurry, Mitch told himself. Like all things, it would come to him sooner or later . . .

A mongrel limped out of the darkness. It was a black Labrador-collie mix and it sat before Mitch and whined for food. Mitch liked dogs, but not dogs that whined. He placed them in the same category as human whiners, which he hated most of all, and told this one to get lost. When the dog did not move, Mitch felt a need to set it straight.

'Ever see that old flick, *This Gun For Hire?* Paramount, 1942. Alan Ladd's first movie. Made him famous. He played this hit-man called Raven, a mean sonofabitch who survived all kinds of rough stuff but got killed in the end 'cause he loved cats.'

The mongrel scratched itself, as if confused.

'What I'm getting' at,' Mitch went on, 'is loners like me and Raven — outcasts in a fantasy world dreamed up by writers never even *held* a gun, let alone fired one — we're supposed to be soft touches for stray animals.' He finished the last bite, held the box to his mouth and drained the salty-sweet juice. 'I'm here to tell you it ain't so. No, sirree. Not even close. I'm no Raven, but I've known a few hit men and I know what makes 'em tick. And it ain't sentimentality. Most of 'em come from dysfunctional homes, like me. They look like ordinary guys, 'cept they got no conscience and a black hole where their heart should be. They're quieter than most folks, too, with silky voices and smiles that'd melt stone. You'd walk right past 'em on the street, or buy 'em a beer in a bar. That is, if you didn't notice their eyes. See, it's their eyes tell the story. They're flat and dead-looking in the center. You know, like a shark's. Only other eyes I ever seen like that belonged to a test pilot.'

The mongrel yawned and chewed at a flea that was biting its tail.

'But wherever these shooters come from, or however they look and act, like me, the one thing we all got in common is we're alone and, truth is, none of us give a fuck if you poor dumb mutts drown, get run over or starve to death. All we care about is ourselves . . . and surviving.'

The mongrel whined again. Mitch, irked because he had hoped the dog had understood him and acquired some backbone, threw the empty box at it. The dog sniffed it and then expressed how it felt about Mitch by pissing on the lid.

'Same to you, pal.' Mitch jumped off the hood. The movement chased the mongrel away. Mitch reached for his Camels. He stuck one in his mouth and deliberately took his time lighting it, thumbing the wheel of his Bic several times before doing it hard enough to make a flame — and in those moments he let his eyes stray up the street.

The black Lincoln Town Car that had followed him from Harrah's to the pawn-shop, where he had pawned Lionel's guns (to keep them out of the law's hands, not to make money), and on throughout the day was still parked there. The dark-tinted windows hid whoever was inside keeping tabs on him, and rather than let them know he had seen them, Mitch got into his car and drove away.

The Town Car gave him a head start before following. The driver then played it smart and let another car get between him and the Dodge. Mitch was not fooled. As he drove, he saw the Lincoln headlights distantly in his rear-view mirror and for the umpteenth time wondered who was following him. And why? Since he was unknown in the area, his tail had to be in some way connected to Lionel, or Lila and Joey. Mitch could have ditched them. But Tahoe was a small area and sooner or later they would catch up with him again, so what was the point? No, the best thing to do was be patient, let them play out their hand and then deal with them.

Okay, Mitch thought as he looked in his rear-view mirror, I'll make it easy for you. You picked me up first at Harrah's, so I'll go back there and see if your boss decides it's time to get in touch with me.

★   ★   ★

In Harrah's casino Claire was losing big. She stood at the craps table, trendy sunglasses hiding her eyes from the glare of the lights, ignoring the jostling throng of bettors about her, throwing the dice with savage abandonment, hoping for an eight that would break her losing streak.

Across the table Mitch won three hundred dollars by betting against Claire. She was fascinating to watch. Easily the most beautiful woman in the casino, her calm expression seldom changed, win or lose. She obviously did not need the money, but Mitch knew it was eating her guts out to keep losing. She was a winner and, like all winners, it killed her when she lost.

Claire rolled the dice again. All the players held their breath as the dice bounced against the backboard. Snake eyes! Claire shrugged, tipped the croupier a twenty-five-dollar chip and headed for the bar.

Mitch cashed his chips in and followed her. She had her back to him and he didn't think she saw him coming. But when he sat down beside her, she took a sip of her drink and, without turning, said: 'You don't give up easily, do you?'

'With a face like mine, honey, would you?'

His comment made her look at him.

'Uh-oh,' he said. 'Careful, now, that looks suspiciously like a smile.'

Claire removed her sunglasses and stared at him with two blue ice cubes. 'What exactly do you want, cowboy?'

'First, I want you to stop callin' me cowboy. I'm not a cowboy and, more importantly, it's an injustice to all the real cowboys.'

'And second?' she said, unfazed.

'You just won me a bundle. Seems only fair I return the favor.'

'Money's one thing I don't need.'

'What do you need?'

'Nothing you can give me.'

'Too bad. We would've looked great waltzing down the aisle.'

'Wait a minute,' Claire said as Mitch started to rise. 'Maybe you *can* help, after all.'

'How?'

'I *could* use some scintillating conversation.'

'Tell me what scintillatin' means and I'll be happy to oblige.'

'A sense of humor. I like that.'

'Enough to buy me a drink?'

Claire hesitated and then pushed the money before her to the bartender. 'Give Mr. Smooth Talker, here, whatever he wants.'

Mitch, knowing he had at least made it to first base, ordered a Coors. 'So, what're we goin' to talk about? All the things we got in common?'

'We don't have murder in common.'

'If you're referring to that punk, Joey, at the motel, that was self-defense.'

'What about your partner, Lionel Banks?'

Mitch instantly went on red alert.

'What about him?'

'On the news they said he was dead and that you were a potential suspect.'

Mitch studied Claire, his expression blank so she could not read what he was thinking.

'They're wrong,' he said quietly. 'Lionel's death was an accident. Ask Sheriff Briggs.'

Claire leaned close and looked directly into his world-weary, yellow-gray eyes. 'Are they wrong about the girl, too?'

'Lila Hendricks?'

'They say you were doing her when she got shot.'

'You think maybe that was politically incorrect?'

'Some people might question your morality.'

'What's sex got to do with morality?'

Claire laughed; a soft husky laugh that Mitch found tantalizing. 'Word around Tahoe is Lila was paying you off.'

'That's a dangerous assumption.'

'Meaning?'

'Maybe I'm not as corrupt as I pretend.'

'Are you?'

'What do you think?'

'I think, Mr. Holliday, you saw a chance to get a freebee. I also think you intended to take Lila back to L.A. all along — which in my eyes makes you a major slime-ball.'

'Guilty as charged.'

'Well, at least you don't deny it. That's worth some points.' Claire studied him a moment. When he didn't wilt under her steely gaze, she dug her long pink nails into the back of Mitch's hand. It hurt like hell but he didn't want her to know, so he smiled as if he were enjoying it.

'We havin' fun yet?'

She removed her hand. 'I just wanted to see if there was blood or ice in your veins.'

'And now that you know?'

'It's time for me to leave.'

'Hey, put it in neutral. Look,' he added when she sat back down, 'it's what I do, huntin' down thieves and bail-jumpers. I go soft and let one go, my reputation goes into the dumpster. Then I'd have to find another line of work and I don't know any other line of work.'

'If you're looking for sympathy,' Claire said, 'you're putting your hand up the wrong skirt.'

Though her expression remained elegantly aloof, her voice sounded so provocative it gave him the courage to say:

'Is that an invitation?' He half-expected to be slapped. When nothing happened, Mitch put his hand on her knee. When she did not push it away, he reached up under her skirt, She still didn't stop him.

'You're full of surprises, lady.'

'Like you said, what does sex have to do with morality?' Picking up her purse, she slid off the stool taking the smell of wet lilacs with her. Mitch started to follow, but she held up a warning finger.

'Don't bother. And don't hit on me again.'

'Why not?'

'Because I don't associate with anyone who coils when he sits.' She walked off.

Disappointed, Mitch watched her leave. *The way she talked*, he thought, *she could wear a pencil-thin mustache, too.* That didn't sit well with him but she seemed so vulnerable, he convinced himself it was just a façade and let it slide.

As Claire walked out the door, Mitch saw two big men at the end of the bar finish their drinks and follow her. He recognized them from before, when he had collared Lila in the casino. They had been standing like fashionable bookends — or 'G.Q. Muscle', as he'd thought then — behind the hot young redhead with the crutches. They were bodyguards, most likely; though whether they were guarding her against trouble or from causing trouble was probably a moot point. And now these two Johnny One-Notes were following his goddess outside. Intrigued, Mitch finished his drink and ambled out after them.

In the hotel parking lot, Mitch heard a stifled scream. He was not surprised; in fact, he had been expecting it. He looked toward the sound. Three figures were struggling among the parked cars. Unhurried, he walked toward them, guessing before he actually saw their faces that it was his goddess and the two men who had followed her.

He was not disappointed. Taggert and Mace had forced Claire to the ground in an attempt to rape her. Mace now held her still while Taggert straddled her. Struggling, she cursed both men.

Mitch approached them, ambling along like a contented bear with its hands in its pockets. Taggert and Mace didn't see him coming. But Claire did and Mitch could see she expected him to rescue her. When he didn't, she begged him to please help her.

Mitch was no Bruce Lee. But he knew what hurt. He kicked Taggert in the kidneys and the big man rolled off Claire, yelping and clutching his back. Mace whirled around to face Mitch who kicked him in the crotch. Mace doubled over, sucking wind. Mitch kneed him in the face. He felt cartilage go and blood spurted. Mace collapsed, grunting. It wasn't kung-fu, or pretty, but it worked. Neither man tried to stop Mitch when he helped Claire up and dusted her off like a new suit.

'You okay?'

'Do I *look* okay?'

'Ask me that when I know you better.'
Behind her, Mitch saw the men stagger
off but didn't try to stop them.

'Just out of interest,' Claire said angrily,
'how long would you have stood there, if I
hadn't asked for help?'

'Depends on how entertaining it was.'

'Some fucking hero you are.'

'You want heroes, lady, go to the
movies.'

She looked puzzled. 'Why're you being
such a jerk all of a sudden?'

'Maybe I don't like being brushed off,'
he said, deciding to hide the real reason.
'Or called a snake.'

'Then why did you bother to come
over?'

'Same reason a moth flies into a flame.'

She studied him with cool blue eyes
and a faintly mocking smile. 'Know what
I think? I think you're not as tough as you
pretend. I think, deep down, under all
that macho swagger you're nothing but a
softie.'

Mitch dug out his Camels and lit up.
'We'd better call the cops.'

'No. No cops.'

'Why not?'

'Buy me a drink instead.'

'Only if you apologize for callin' me a snake.'

Claire smiled suggestively and groped him. 'How about part snake?'

Mitch had to laugh. And before the idiot in him could say anything to drive this goddess away, he led her back into the hotel.

★   ★   ★

They sat at a corner table in the lounge, drinking stingers. Now that they had broken the ice and he thought he was beginning to understand her, he expected her to lose some of her appeal, her vulnerability. Instead, she seemed even more helpless, more desirable, and Mitch felt himself drowning in those big, pale-blue-but-no-longer-aloof eyes.

Suddenly in his mind he heard a deep, gloomy voice, Lionel's voice, talking to him. Mitch visualized the two of them on an all-night stakeout way the hell out in the boonies; sitting there in the dark in

Mitch's old Chevy across the street from a pink stucco duplex inside which some horny banker's wife was being humped by her Mercedes mechanic; sitting there with the radio banging out oldies-but-goodies, Mitch washing down glazed doughnuts with black vanilla-nut coffee from 7-Eleven, Lionel chewing on Trailmix Bars and drinking Evian water bought at Mrs. Goochie's. They had been talking about chicks and falling in love and getting married and Lionel said with an air of authority that he always possessed when he spoke of women: 'Listen, numb-nuts. You ever meet a chick you can't stay away from? Picture her early in the morning, you know, hair all messy, no frigging makeup and sitting naked on the toilet. It'll turn you off quicker than herpes.'

Mitch tried to picture Claire in that pose. But he couldn't get past her perfect features, dazzling smile, and long hair that seemed to have a life of its own, constantly falling over one eye like a golden waterfall.

'Penny?' he vaguely heard her say.

'I was thinkin' . . . wondering if you'd

like to come back to my place.'

Claire put her nose inches from Mitch's and looked into his eyes. 'I was wrong about you, Mr. Holliday.'

'Is that a yes or a no?' When she did not answer, he said: 'How were you wrong?'

'I thought you were smart.'

'What changed your mind?'

'In my book, smart guys don't get involved with women like me.'

'What-kind-is-that-he-asked?'

'Vulnerable.'

Mitch smiled and in an exaggerated tough-guy voice, growled: ''Then she'd come along, like school was out.''

'Robert Mitchum describing Jane Greer in *Out of the Past*.'

'See. We do have somethin' in common. We both watch old movies.'

'We both masturbate, too, but don't get steamed up about our future.'

'Vulnerable *and* tough,' Mitch said, 'Man, that's an intriguing combination. Makes me want to know more about you.'

'Trust me, Mr. Holliday. You don't want to know anything about me. So, do yourself a favor. Stay away from me. I'm bad news.' Downing her drink, she walked out.

Mitch felt a light go out inside him. He looked at the bartender, who stood watching him while rinsing glasses, said: 'Should've seen the one I kept.'

The bartender gave Mitch a sarcastic 'yeah, ri-ight' look and turned away.

10

Mitch lay, fully clothed, on the bed in his motel room wolfing down a pepperoni and sausage pizza and drinking a Coors while watching the Raymond Chandler classic, *Farewell, My Lovely*. It was the RKO version made in 1944, and critics had called it a minor masterpiece. Mitch had seen the movie at least twenty times and knew the dialogue by heart. On-screen Dick Powell was talking to himself and Mitch mimicked him:

'Okay, Marlowe, I said to myself. You're a tough guy. You've been sapped twice, choked, beaten silly with a gun, shot in the arm until you're crazy as a couple of waltzing mice. Now let's see you do something really tough — like putting your pants on.'

Mitch chuckled, took bite of pizza and swigged it down with beer. As he belched and continued watching the movie, he had a strange feeling something was about to go wrong. The premonition made him look around. The room was dark save for the violet glow of the television that cast eerie flickering shadows on the walls. He listened and heard the traffic passing along the street outside the motel. Dismissing the feeling as indigestion, he glanced at the bedside clock. The glowing red numerals showed it was: 2:08 a.m.

There was a knock. He knew then he had not been wrong.

He also knew who it was. He had been expecting her, in fact, ever since the Lincoln Town Car that tailed him back to his motel had driven off.

'Door's open,' he called out.

Claire entered, bathed in moonlight. Her hair was loose and she looked radiant in a mauve ski-suit gleaming with zippers. Mitch felt her presence rush into his mind like a favorite memory. He wanted to say something warm and sensitive, something that would set the mood for what he hoped was about to happen between them. But Mitch and sensitivity were strangers, and he heard himself saying:

'Little late for school, aren't you?'

'I lost track of time.'

'Oh, poor baby. What happened, Daddy take away your Rolex?'

'Cute. Now, are you going to invite me in or not?'

'Sure — after you explain how you found me.'

'I called your press agent.'

Mitch frowned. 'I'll make a deal with you: I'll quit talkin' like Dick Powell if you'll quit actin' like Barbara Payton.'

'Ouch!' Claire looked hurt. 'You're comparing me to that boozy blonde?'

'Lauren Bacall then, if that'll make you feel better. Either way, we both need to get a life and stop livin' vicariously in the forties. Now, we got a deal or not?'

'Deal. And to answer your question about how I found you,' she went on, 'I saw your room key, first time we met.'

Mitch remembered that he had indeed set his room key, with its green plastic address tag, on the bar at their first meeting.

'You got a good memory.'

'That mean you're going to invite me in?'

'Could I keep you out?'

'Obviously,' she said, stung, 'I made a mistake in coming here.'

'No, wait,' he said as she turned to go. 'I was just kiddin'. Come on in.' He watched as she took one step into the room, stopped and looked at him.

'Beer's all I got,' he began. 'But — '

'Ask me what color my panties are.'

''Scuse me?'

'Ask me what color my panties are.'

'What color are your panties?'

'Same color as my nail polish.'

'You're not wearing any.'

Claire smiled, locked the door and joined him on the bed. The smell of wet lilacs tantalized his senses as she came close. Mitch tried to resist her, but it was useless.

Grabbing her, he pulled her close and took her.

★   ★   ★

Afterward, Mitch lay on the bed watching Claire standing naked at the window, her head cocked sideways a little so she could see through a crack in the blinds. Her tanned body, even in the shadowy half-light, was so flawless it could have been a statue.

Mitch realized he had never seen anyone so damned beautiful. She was a little crazy, of course, but then he had never had dealings with a goddess before and maybe it came with the territory. Anyway, he was not complaining; he just wanted to make her happy so she would stay.

'Was it as good for you as it was for me?'

'Absolutely,' Claire lied.

'Then why do I feel like I didn't knock you off the Richter scale?'

'Macho insecurity?'

Mitch chuckled, 'Sure got me pegged.'

Claire didn't say anything for a moment but kept her eyes riveted on the parking lot outside. Then, without turning from the window, she said: 'Your first name — what's it short for, Mitchum?'

'Uh-uh. Mitchell. After my grandfather. But it just as easily could've been Mitchum, the way grandma felt about him.' He smiled at his thoughts. 'She had the biggest crush on the guy. Told me she'd seen every movie he ever made.'

'My grandfather named me after Claire Trevor for the same reason. Said he fell in love with her in *Key Largo*.'

'No kiddin'?' Mitch grinned. 'I told you we had a lot in common.'

'I doubt that. But if you're right, I recommend we both do what you suggested earlier: get new lives.'

'As far as mine goes, I'd agree with you —'

'But because I'm rich and beautiful, I couldn't possibly be unhappy, right?'

She said it with such venom, Mitch hesitated before answering.

'Are you tryin' to tell me your life sucks as much as mine?'

If she heard him, she didn't show it. 'If I'd lived back in the forties,' she said wistfully, 'know who I'd want to be?'

'Rita Hayworth?'

'Rosie the Riveter. I'm serious,' she said as he laughed. 'My nanny, Mrs. Toberman, worked swing-shift at Douglas when she was young. Used to tell me all about how great it was, and what a sense of accomplishment she felt by knowing she was actually doing something to help win the war. Said everyone worked their butts off, but it didn't matter because they felt like a team, you know, one big happy family. And after they got off work, even though they were exhausted, they all went dancing and drinking and then went home and fell into bed. Said also it was so much fun living with these two other gals who worked alongside her and how they all lived together in this green-and-white bungalow near the pier in Santa Monica — '

She broke off as, between the blinds, she saw the Lincoln Town Car pull into the motel. Mace and Taggert, dressed like ads for Armani and Boss, got out and entered the office. Claire turned from the window, picked up her ski-suit, boots and purse from the floor, and started for the bathroom.

Mitch stopped her. 'Not leaving, are you?'

'I was thinking about it. Why?'

'Something's been chewin' on me.'

'Can't it wait until I get my clothes on?'

'Only take a second.'

'All right, but hurry it up. I'm f-freezing.'

'How come you changed your mind?'

'About what?'

'Me?'

'What, you're looking for compliments now?'

'Okay. Forget that. How come you didn't want me to call the cops and have those clowns who jumped you picked up?'

'Did you ask Lila this many questions?'

'Lila didn't have any secrets.'

'How boring.'

'Yeah, but she gave great head.'

Claire laughed huskily. 'If you must know, smart ass, I didn't want the cops involved because I'm trying to keep a low profile. That's why I sound like Barbara Payton. I've been staying home all week watching old movies. Okay?'

'Works for me.'

Claire leaned close and kissed Mitch until his toes curled. 'Now I have a question for you.'

'Shoot.'

'Why are all the men I like broke or bums?'

'Man,' he said as she headed into the bathroom. 'You sure know how to boost a guy's ego.'

There was a knock on the door, Mitch pulled on his pants. 'You don't have a husband, do you?' he called out.

No answer came from the bathroom.

Mitch knew what was coming next. He also knew that sometimes you had to take some hits to get some answers. So, removing his partial bridge, he put it in his pocket and opened the door.

Instantly, Taggert's fist slammed him in the mouth. Mitch went down. He curled into a protective ball and stayed that way until Mace stopped kicking him. Taggert, meanwhile, had kicked in the bathroom door, seen the open window through which Claire had escaped, and returned beside Mitch. 'Okay, where'd the bitch go?'

'You tell me.'

'We could beat it out of you.'

'You could try,' Mitch said. 'But all you'd get is sore knuckles and a wild guess.'

'Tough guy, huh?'

'Nope. But one look at this face should tell you I've taken enough beatings to know the score.'

Mace and Taggert swapped questioning looks and came to a silent agreement.

Mace grinned mirthlessly at Mitch. 'You're mine,' he said, and pistol-whipped him until he was senseless. Then Armani and Boss left.

11

The Golden Princess was Tahoe's most recent luxury high-rise hotel. It towered over all the others. It had the biggest casino and, as its commercials bragged, every window had a breathtaking view of the lake.

Tonight, a corporate helicopter was parked on the roof. Its company logo read: BENCO INDUSTRIES. Nearby, Mace stood bundled up against the chilling wind, talking on a cell phone to his boss, Edgar Bennett. When he was finished, he turned to the pilot beside him.

'Warm up the bird. The Old Man's ready to go.'

The pilot climbed into the chopper, buckled up, flipped on the ignition, and the rotors slowly started whirling. Mace entered the roof elevator and descended one floor to the penthouse suite.

There, Edgar Bennett was pacing

behind his desk as he raged into the telephone. He was a short, immaculately dressed man of fifty-two with graying brown hair and the features of an aging Soap star. A ruthless egomaniac, he bullied everyone he met and went out of his way to destroy anyone who stood up to him. If he had a good side, and few thought he did, it was his hatred of drugs and drug dealers and his compassion for anyone who wanted but couldn't afford an education. BENCO Industries was famous for its huge donations to schools in impoverished areas and for foundations that funded poverty-level education in general. His business enemies, which included almost everyone, downplayed Edgar Bennett's generosity, claiming that, hey — what's the big deal? If BENCO didn't donate the money, it would go to taxes anyway — an accusation that incensed Bennett, and one he fervently denied.

Watching him now, barking orders into a speaker phone while he gathered up folded blueprints of a ski resort and stuffed them into his briefcase, one realized he was a human dynamo fueled by a single-minded obsession to dominate everyone and everything: the ultimate control freak on the ultimate power trip.

'Don't give me that bullshit!' he shouted into the phone. 'I pay you and your overpriced team of pussy-faced litigators for results, not excuses!' He listened a moment, veins in his neck and forehead bulging, then yelled: 'I don't give a rat's ass about the threat to the Canada goose. And the only goddamn deer I want to see are those draped over the hood of some rednecked, card-carrying member of the NRA!' The voice on the line tried to explain something, but Edgar Bennett angrily cut him off. 'So, get an injunction against the bastards. I don't care what it costs or who the hell you have to bribe. Just do it! Every day those mealy-mouthed animal-lovers block us from clearing the land costs BENCO a half-million dollars!'

He punched the 'off' button on the speaker phone, jammed the last docu-ment into his briefcase, slammed the lid and tossed the case to Taggert who stood nearby like a fashionably dressed guard-dog.

Across the large office, with its private elevator, custom furniture and windows all around with views of the lake, forests and ski-slopes, Elaina looked up from the jigsaw puzzle she was working on. The puzzle depicted the ancient walled city of Jerusalem, and was complete save for a section of the Dome of the Rock, the missing pieces forming the shape of a cross.

'What's the matter, Popsy?' Her taunting little-girl voice was slurred by liquor. 'Problems?'

Claire turned from the bar where she was fixing herself a drink and gave her sister a warning look.

Elaina ignored her and smiled sweetly at her stepfather. 'Can it be that some poor peon actually objects to your buying up the whole world?' She giggled and sucked her thumb. 'Why, the nerve of those ungrateful peasants.'

'Shut up,' Edgar Bennett told her. 'One more word out of you and I'll — '

'What, have me locked up in your

favorite dungeon?'

'Elaina — sweetie, knock it off.'

Again, Elaina ignored her sister. 'It's too bad we aren't still living in the Roman days,' she went on, 'then you could have me flogged and crucified or fed to the lions.'

Edgar Bennett erupted. 'That's it! I've had enough of you, you fucking Jesus freak! You're going away for good!' He charged toward her.

Claire quickly cut him off. 'Edgar, she's drunk . . .'

'Get out of my goddamn way.'

'Please . . . let it go. For me?'

It was a struggle, but gradually the veins in his neck and forehead faded and he regained control. 'Okay, but get-her-out-of-here. Now!'

Claire turned to Taggert. 'Help my sister to her room, please.'

Taggert looked at Edgar Bennett, who nodded. Taggert tossed the briefcase to Mace, grabbed the crutches and handed them to Elaina.

'Why, thank you, lover.' Elaina pulled herself up by the edge of the table. Then supporting herself with one crutch, she rubbed the tip of the other suggestively between her thighs. 'For being so sweet, maybe I'll let you do me later. Again.'

Edgar Bennett somehow controlled his anger until Taggert and Elaina had left the room. Then he began raging at Claire. 'When I get back,' he yelled, 'I'm having that crazy little nympho committed. Save your breath,' he said as she started to protest. 'This time, I mean it. She's as good as buried.' He started for the elevator, Mace hurrying ahead of him.

Claire said softly: 'What if I said yes?'

Edgar Bennett turned and looked at her. 'You'd do that just to keep that little nutcase free?'

'If that's what it takes, yes.'

'Maybe I don't want you that way.'

'What difference does it make what way it is, so long as you have me?'

'That depends on how much of you I have.'

Claire moved close, put her arms about his neck and kissed him passionately on the lips.

'That enough?'

Edgar Bennett studied her, ever suspicious.

'After all this time, why now?'

'Let's say . . . you've finally won me over.'

'In my dreams.'

'Does that mean you don't want me?'

'It means I don't trust you.'

'I don't blame you for that. But I wish you'd give me the time to earn your trust. I think you'd find me worth it.' She pressed against him and gave him another steamy kiss. 'Come back to me soon, darling.'

Edgar Bennett nodded, still suspicious of her sincerity, and entered the elevator with Mace. The door slid shut.

Claire walked to the door and spat on it. She watched her spittle running down the door, thinking: I hope you crash and burn to death, you perverted little bastard!

★ ★ ★

In her luxurious pink-and-white suite down the hall Elaina slowly, tantalizingly undressed in front of Taggert.

'What do you think of my new tattoo?' she asked, fingering the tattoo of Christ on the cross that adorned her smooth white stomach between her breasts and naval.'

'I think,' Taggert replied, 'I'd keep that puppy covered up around your father, if I were you.'

'He's not my father,' she hissed. 'He's Satan posing as a human cockroach! And if you ever want to screw me again, you'll remember that.'

Taggert lost his bluster. 'Okay, okay, don't boil your water. I'm just tryin' to save you from gettin' more grief.'

'Very well, I forgive you,' she said, calming. Then, as he sat on the bed and unbuttoned his shirt: 'Don't forget, lover, call me Jesus while you're doing me.'

'Yeah, yeah,' he said, realizing she was getting whackier by the minute. 'Anythin' you say, baby — '

A connecting door flew open and Claire raged into the bedroom. 'Get out!' she screamed at Taggert.

Elaina giggled and sucked her thumb.

100

'Sorry, Tag'. Guess you'll have to go it solo tonight.'

Taggert grabbed his jacket and stormed out. Claire kicked the door shut behind him and turned on her sister.

'Are you out of your freaking mind?'

'I believe that's the general consensus.'

Claire lost it. She grabbed Elaina and shook her hard. 'Don't mess with me, little sister!'

Elaine sat up, shaken but also defiant. 'Just 'cause you're pissed off at Popsy, don't take it out on me.'

'Then snap out of it. This is serious.'

'I hate serious,' said Elaina, her eyes two green saucers in her angelic face. 'Where's the fun in being crazy if you can't do crazy things?'

Claire wanted to slap her. But she knew that was what Elaina wanted, why she was goading her, to be punished, and Claire wasn't about to appease her.

Teeth gritted, she said: 'Don't you realize you're one step away from being committed.'

'I'm *already* committed.' Elaina gestured drunkenly about her. 'Popsy just hasn't gotten around to padding the walls yet . . . ' Suddenly, her defiance melted away. She burst into tears and buried her face in the pillow. 'Oh-h God,' she wept, 'I want him dead so badly.'

Claire softened. She sat on the bed and gently stroked her sister's long gold-red hair. 'Don't worry, sweetie, it'll happen.'

'No, it won't. It'll never happen.' Elaine rolled over and gripped her sister's wrists. 'The bastard will go on living and torturing us forever, and every time we come up with a new way to kill him, some fluky thing will happen, like it did this time with Lionel — '

'That was just an unlucky accident — '

'No, no, it was an act of God, a warning; Jesus told me so.'

'Stop it, Elaina! Don't start with that religious nonsense again.'

'It's not nonsense! Why won't you believe me? Jesus *did* tell me, in this dream I had and when I woke up there were holes in my palms, you know, just like in His hands after they took Him down from the cross — '

'Oh-my-God, when's it going to stop — '

'You don't believe me, here, look for yourself, see — ' Elaina held out her hands, palms up, to Claire — 'they're still there.'

Claire looked and saw a small round red welt, resembling a birthmark, in the center of each palm. She was not sure why, but her stomach turned over uneasily.

'Now do you believe me?'

Claire didn't know what to believe. To help maintain her sanity, she pulled the covers over the front of her sister, hiding the crucifix tattoo and both her hands.

'Those are just marks, not holes. They could have come from anything.'

'But they didn't, they *didn't*, the holes caused them, and . . . oh God, God, why won't you let me die like I'm supposed to?'

'Stop saying that, sweetie — '

Elaina wasn't listening. Pounding the pillow with both fists, she raged: 'I hate You, God, and You too, Jesus, oh, how I hate You both for not letting me die with momma . . . ' She stopped punching the pillow and buried her face in it, her sobbing increasing until her whole body shook.

Claire stroked her hair. 'Shhhh, sweetie, shhhh, it'll be okay, I promise.'

But nothing could stop Elaina. She sobbed and sobbed. And with every sob, Claire's expression grew grimmer. Her mind churned as she searched for a way to kill their stepfather.

12

Across town in his squalid little motel room Mitch sat on the bed gingerly feeling the welts on his head caused by Mace's pistol-whipping.

The manager hovered anxiously nearby, watching him.

'Want me to call the sheriff, Mr. Holliday?'

'No, he's had enough laughs for one night.' Mitch slowly got to his feet, back and ribs aching, and waited for the room to stop spinning before he said: 'The woman who was with me — you see her drive off?'

'What woman?'

'Memory loss is a sad thing.' Mitch grabbed the manager's nose and twisted, hard. 'But you'll be happy to know it can be cured.'

The manager yelped. 'I never saw her leave, I swear, but my wife, Maude, said she called.'

'When?'

'Few minutes ago. That's why I came and knocked on your door. She said I'd find a snake in here.' He looked nervously about. 'It's against motel rules to keep pets in the room, you know.'

Mitch laughed to himself. 'This woman, did she say anythin' else?'

'No. I mean, yeah, she give Maude a phone number to write down.' He handed Mitch a note. 'Said if you hadn't gotten any smarter by tomorrow, call her.'

Mitch grinned and started out.

'Hey, what about the snake?'

'It's okay,' Mitch said. 'I'm takin' it with me.'

★ ★ ★

Sheriff Briggs drove into the sheriff sub-station lot and parked his car beside Mitch's blue compact. Both men rolled down their windows so they could talk.

'What's so important we couldn't yak over the phone?'

'Ever watch old war movies, Sheriff?'

'Only if Duke Wayne's in 'em. Why?'

''Loose lips sink ships.''

'That's it?' Sheriff Briggs said irritably. 'You dragged me away from a warm fire and my buddy Jack Daniels to quote me a goddamn World War Two slogan?'

'You got a leak in your office. I wanted you to know about it before I got blamed.'

'For what?'

'Someone went public about Lionel's death and it wasn't me.'

'How d'you know that?'

'Apparently it was on the news.'

'Damn.' The sheriff methodically mulled things over. 'Those CHP guys must've blabbed.'

'What about your own department?'

'As of midnight, all my deputies are out with the 'blue flu.'' He started his car. 'I'll make some calls. Get back to you.'

'How're the hemorrhoids?'

'Fire in the hole, son. Fire in the hole.'

13

Mitch followed Shoreline Drive around the lake. The morning sky was overcast and there was rain in the air, making everything damp and gloomy. He passed a little convenience store and turned down a dirt side-road. Ahead, built among the dark green pines, stood an expensive redwood-rock-and-glass cottage with a million-dollar view of the lake. Parked behind it was the black Lincoln Town car.

Mitch smiled to himself as he pulled up beside it. What he had surmised earlier, when he'd first seen the Lincoln tailing him, had proved to be true. Again, all he needed to do was be patient and wait. Feeling pretty good about himself, he got out of the Dodge and stretched the morning chill from his bones.

A voice called out his name from above. He looked up and saw Claire waving to him from the sundeck. 'Hang on,' she told him. 'Be right with you.' She disappeared indoors to put on her coat and gloves.

They walked slowly through the woods. Glimpses of the lake showed pale and leaden between the pines. Squirrels darted across their path. Deer tracks showed in the damp earth. Claire seemed more relaxed than Mitch had ever seen her. She even slipped her arm through his as she talked, telling him how much she loved it up here — the solitude, the scenery, incredible fresh air — and when questioned by Mitch, replied that the cottage belonged to friends of hers in Pasadena, the Grogans.

'That where you're from — City of Roses?'

'San Marino, actually. But — ' She suddenly stopped, unable to hide it any longer and lifted her eyes guiltily to his. 'Mitch, darling, I'm sorry I ran out on you.'

'Forget it.'

'I can't. I'm no candidate for Goodie-Two-Shoes, but leaving you to Taggert and Mace, that's reaching a new kind of low even for me. They could've killed you.'

'Then why'd you split?'

'I was scared . . . ' She clung to him, her cheek cold against his and the ever-familiar smell of wet lilacs behind her ears. 'You can't imagine how frightening it is to have men chasing you, trying to drag you back to a place you hate more than anything.'

'School's really that bad?

'Please don't make fun of me, Mitch. I know I look like I'm Miss Cool-and-Calm, one of those rich, elegant bitches who can take care of herself, but that's nothing but a stupid façade. Inside, I'm scared to death.'

He had difficulty believing her. But when he felt her trembling in his arms, he melted.

'Sorry. I didn't mean to step on your feelings . . . '

They walked through the dark, solemn pines in silence, hand-in-hand now. A blue jay suddenly swooped down in front of them, its indignant screeching startling them out of their thoughts.

'These cretins — why they after you?'

'They're watchdogs. My stepfather pays them to make sure Elaina and I don't go anywhere alone.'

'Overly protective type, huh?'

'Try insanely jealous. God, he hates it when other men even *look* at us. Me, especially.'

'Sounds like a real lovable guy.'

'There aren't enough obscenities in Webster's to describe him.'

'Isn't there anyone else you can turn to — your mom, for instance?'

'My mother's dead. Edgar — that's my stepfather, Edgar Bennett — had her killed.'

Mitch stopped in mid-stride. 'Edgar Bennett? As in Edgar Vincent Bennett, the billionaire developer?'

Claire nodded. 'You know him?'

'Oh sure, we play poker every Friday night.'

'That's not as far-fetched as you may think. Edgar has lots of tough guys on his payroll. Men who'd do anything for him — including, kill my mother.'

'Got any steak to go with that sizzle?'

111

'I can't prove it, if that's what you mean. Edgar's too clever for that. According to the D.A., who's in Edgar's pocket, it was just another tragic boating accident.'

'You're free, white and twenty-one — why stick around?'

'Because I'd be running out on the one person I love more than anything, my kid sister.' Claire let go of Mitch's hand and looked between the tall, wet pines at the lake. The calm water glinted like pewter. She went away somewhere dark and uncomfortable, and when she returned a few moments later she sounded full of pain.

'Poor baby's a cripple, physically and mentally. She has these delusions, thinks Jesus talks to her and inflicts marks on her when he's angry with her — '

'Marks? What kind of marks?'

'Red marks, in the middle of her palms. You know, like Christ had after the Resurrection.'

'You're kiddin'? You ever seen 'em?'

'Once.'

'And?'

Claire shrugged. 'There wasn't anything special about them, if that's what you're asking.' As if convincing herself, she added: 'They certainly weren't made by nails.'

'How you think they got there?'

'Knowing Elaina, she probably made them herself, maybe even burned herself just so people would believe her story.' Claire paused, distraught, then said wearily: 'Poor sweetie needs special care and therapy, the kind I can't afford to give her. Edgar knows that, all too well. That's why he's arranged it so we can't get our hands on any money. As a result, Elaina and I are virtually prisoners in our own home.'

Thunder rumbled overhead, and it began to drizzle.

Looking skyward, Claire sighed, 'We better be getting home,' and headed back to the cottage without waiting for him. Mitch hesitated, troubled by his thoughts and his growing impulse to help her, then hurried after her.

★　★　★

By nightfall, the rain was bouncing off the cottage windows. Occasionally, raindrops came down the chimney, making the roaring fire sizzle. Claire fixed a couple of rare New York's, a spinach salad, baked potatoes and creamed onions, while Mitch uncorked a bottle of Stag's Leap cabernet. Both were famished and they sat on stools at the kitchen counter, wolfing everything down, listening to soft jazz and watching the rain fall.

'I hope this helps make up for what Taggert and Mace did to you.'

'Lady, in my work the hits come hard and often, but never with steak and wine. Believe me, kiddo, you're forgiven. Big time.'

Claire smiled; and studied him thoughtfully.

'Why the look?'

'You're an enigma, you know that.'

''Cause I forgive you?'

'Because you don't seem like a person who'd — well, you know, do what you do.'

'Bring 'em back alive?' Mitch shrugged his powerful, sloping shoulders. 'There are worse gigs. Some folks might figure it's a step down from being a P.I. but — '

'Is that what you were — a private investigator?'

'Till the D.A.'s office yanked my ticket, yeah.' He saw her questioning look. 'Why'd-they-do-that-she-asked?'

'You don't have to tell me, not if you don't want to.'

'It's not exactly top secret.' Mitch paused, making sure he had control of the anger he knew would come once he got started on the subject, and then said: 'I killed a cop. A detective in vice, name of James Danville.'

'That must've gone over big.'

'Like a cold hand between your legs.'

'I'm sure you had good reason.'

'No such thing. Cops get all bent out of shape you whack one of their brethren, no matter what reason — which in my case was kill or be killed.'

'Why'd he want to kill you?'

'Guy was a sadistic prick; got his kicks beatin' up hookers. One of them, a friend of mine, ended up in the hospital. I returned the favor, and after he got back on his feet he spread the word he was gonna run me out of Dodge.' Mitch sighed, the incident as clear now as it was two years ago when it happened; clearer even; more maddening, and always the flood of anger and frustration rising inside him. 'When he couldn't do that, he tried to kill me.'

'If he was in the wrong, why'd the Department come down on you?'

'Danville was smarter than I gave him credit for. He fixed it to look like I was part of a money launderin' ring and somehow managed to deposit a shit-load of cash into my bank account. I was sentenced to eighteen months but with time off for good behavior, I ended up doin' a year on the farm, and after I got out the D.A.'s office said no, no, no, when I tried to renew my ticket.'

'Sounds unfair.'

'You want fair, go to Pomona, as they say in Orange County.'

Claire sipped her wine before asking: 'Can't you hire a lawyer and fight back? Prove you're innocent?'

'Nobody's innocent.'

'That's pretty cynical.'

'Hey, everybody's got dirt on them. All you have to do is dig deep enough . . . '

'I wish that were true about Edgar . . . ' Claire looked at the rain-spattered window. 'I'd give a year of my life to get something on him — something that would force the bastard to let Elaina and me go.' She sighed regretfully and tapped her pink nails against her wine glass. 'But that's just wishful thinking. Edgar's untouchable. And so long as he believes there's a chance he can force me to marry him, he'll never let us go.'

'Whoa, back up the bus, lady. Marry-his-own-stepdaughter?'

'Sick, isn't it? But it's been his goal all along.'

'Then, why'd he marry your mom?'

'To get her money. Once he had control of that, his real agenda came to the surface.' She paused, finding it difficult to continue. Finally, above the drumming of the rain, she said: 'He played the doting husband, so nobody would be suspicious. But all the time he was waiting like a hungry spider. Then one day when my mother and sister were out on the lake, racing around having fun, one of his men rigged an explosion . . . Mom died instantly, but Elaina, she by some miracle was thrown clear of the boat. Two water-skiers found her a few minutes later, floating in the water. Her back was broken and — I can't remember the medical term for it, but basically the nerves at the base of her spine were all shot . . . ' She broke off, tears coming, unable to continue.

Mitch, hurting for her, pressed a big, gnarly hand over hers. He tried to think of something comforting to say, but everything he thought of sounded corny and insincere. So, he waited, emotions held in check, deep down wishing he could help her.

After an agonizing silence, Claire sniffed back her tears and said bitterly, 'Depraved bastard, I only wish I had the guts to kill him. I'd snuff out his life in a second and never give it another thought. But, unfortunately, it isn't in me. I could never kill anyone. Christ, I can't even step on a damn cockroach . . . '

'Take it easy,' Mitch said gently.

'Sorry . . . ' Claire tried to calm down. 'That's Edgar for you. He brings out the worst in everyone. Oh God, dear God, how I hate him!' Jumping up, she ran down the hall to her bedroom. Mitch heard the door slam behind her, followed by muffled sobbing.

14

Now what, Mitch wondered. Should he leave Claire alone to cry it out or go in there and try to help her through it? Conflicting emotions battled inside him. He wished he were more sensitive, but hard knocks and mean streets had punched it out of him; had taught him to bury his feelings so deep, he couldn't reach them. *Tough guys don't cry, his old man had hammered into him when he was a kid. Jesus effing Christ, you wanna be known as a damn crybaby? You think crying ever solved anythin'? Hell, no. Don't complain, don't explain. Nobody's said it better and nobody ever will, not in a million years. You wanna be a man, you suck it up. Take your goddamn medicine in silence. You got that, kiddo? Goddamn little wimp. Come home cryin' again and I'll give you somethin' to really cry for. Now dry your eyes and get your sorry ass out of here 'fore I get take off my belt'n tan it black'n blue.*

The boy, Mitch, ashamed, ran from the room and stood in the dim hall on trembling legs, sniffing back his tears and vowing never to cry again, no matter what.

And he hadn't. But as years piled on, and he had found himself going through women, good and bad, he'd gradually realized that being tough and having no feelings came with a price; you missed out on heartache but also on love as well; and as you grew older, got within shouting distance of the big Five-O and took stock of your life, you had to wonder if you had gone about this emotionless crap the right way. By then, of course, it was too late to change. You were what you were and you did what you did and kept quiet about it.

But wishing sometimes, at night mostly, when it was dark and the bed empty and you couldn't sleep and tried to laugh off loneliness as a preferable alternative to nagging, but knowing, if not admitting it, that bullshit was the only thing the old man had given you and that if you had it to do all over again, you might remember how before your mother died she finally saw through his bullying ways and at last got it right when she was lying there in the county hospital, paler than the sheets and eyes yellow with jaundice, the cancer having eaten up everything inside that worked; but still not complaining, never complaining, but whispering in his ear *'don't listen to him, Mitch, honey. He's dead mean and he'll die with a cigar and a bottle of red his only friends.' And sure enough, that's how they found him; the hotel clerk, a wino himself, smelling smoke and rushing up there, yelling fire, fire! and inside the smoke-filled room finding the flea-infested mattress burning, in smoldering flames, having caught on fire when the cigar butt fell from the derelict's limp, drunken fingers; and the best part, no one bothering to show up at his funeral, not even Mitch, who hadn't spoken to the bitter old wino in years and wouldn't have even known he was dead if someone at the coroner's office hadn't finally remembered there was a son, Mitchell, they thought his name was, who was either a cop or a private ticket, and used their computers to track him down.*

As if it really mattered, Mitch thought then and now. But also thinking *do it for her, the mother who adored you but, thanks to the old man's belligerence, never had the son she wanted, could love; do it for her and at the same time maybe break the cycle, the rules, and show a little tenderness. It can't kill you and maybe, just maybe, it might be that first step to building a genuine relationship with not just another human being, which was hard enough, but with a woman you never thought existed outside your imagination.*

Mitch forced himself to get up and plod to the bedroom door. He stood there several moments, listening to the muffled tears, then he knocked and said gruffly: 'You okay in there?'

No answer.

'Claire, answer me. You okay?'

Again, no answer. So be it, he thought. He had at least *tried* to be understanding. That, by itself, was a first. He took his hand from the doorknob and headed back to the kitchen. On the way, as he crossed the big living room with its bearskin rugs and blazing fire going to waste, Mitch noticed the jigsaw puzzle on a card table in the corner. He went and looked at it. The puzzle was almost finished. It showed Lake Tahoe under a blue summer sky and surrounded by pine-clad mountains. Knowing at first glance it wouldn't match but doing it anyway, so later he'd never wonder if he made a mistake, he dug out the piece of puzzle that Lionel had given him and compared it to the scene. It did not fit anywhere. Satisfied, Mitch returned the piece to his wallet and continued on into the kitchen, where he started gathering up the dinner dishes.

Outside, the rain slackened. Mitch thought the drops falling on the window looked like a dying man's tears.

15

Twenty minutes later Claire emerged from the bedroom. She had washed her face, fixed her hair and makeup, and except for a slight puffiness about her eyes, no one would have known she had been crying.

She came up quietly behind Mitch, who was stacking the dirty plates into the dishwasher, put her arms around his neck and nuzzled his ear. He had seen her reflection in the rain-streaked window over the sink, so he was not startled. He turned within her arms and faced her, saying as gently as he could:

'What can I do to help?'

'That's sweet of you. But there's nothing you or anyone else can do. Edgar holds all the aces and he knows it.' Reaching up on tiptoe, she kissed him, a tender lingering kiss that gradually grew passionate. He knew the time was right then and, picking her up in his arms, he carried her into the bedroom and, for the first time in his life, actually made love to a woman.

*   *   *

Outside, the rain stopped and a full moon smiled through the clouds. It lit up the whole night, painting everything silver.

On the highway, a gray Mercedes limousine with BENCO 1 license plates was parked on the shoulder overlooking the cottage. Mace sat dozing behind the wheel; Taggert snored beside him. But in the back seat, Elaina was awake and looking through binoculars at the window of Claire's bedroom. The bedside lamp was on. By its light Elaina could see Mitch and her sister making love. She smiled and sucked her thumb. Everything was going according to plan.

'C'mon,' she said, shaking Taggert awake. 'Take me to the airport.'

*   *   *

In the middle of the night some innate sense of danger pervaded Mitch's senses.

He opened his eyes and saw Claire silhouetted against the moon hanging in the window. She stood beside the bed, naked, a strange, dreamy look on her face, holding his big, heavy .45 in both hands. It was pointed at him and as calmly as he could, he said:

'Careful, that puppy goes off real easy.'

Claire smiled, the kind of smile wolves smile before they eat you, and raised the gun until it was level with his chest.

Mitch tried to laugh it off. 'Okay, kitten, stop playin' games.'

She ignored him. Very slowly she turned the gun around and aimed it at her own head.

Mitch started sweating. 'Jesus, Claire, cut it out! You want to blow your head off?'

If she heard him, she showed no sign of it. She slowly squeezed the trigger. He grasped for the gun, too late. The gun went off. Mitch heard her scream as the bullet burned her flesh and then she collapsed onto the floor.

He panicked. Was Fate screwing with him again, letting him find a woman he cared for and then yanking her away just to show who was boss? He leaped out of bed, yelling her name, asking her if she was okay, over and over. Claire didn't answer. She lay still on the floor in a pool of moonlight. Mitch cuddled her against him, praying she wasn't dead as he saw blood running down between her breasts.

'You okay . . . ? Claire! Claire, for Chrissake, answer me — are you all right?'

Claire came back from wherever she'd been, opened her eyes and looked at Mitch as if seeing him for the first time.

'W-What happened?'

'You shot yourself, what happened!'

'Shot myself?'

'Yeah . . . ' He checked her wound, a jagged crease on her left shoulder. 'Few inches over and you would've been history. *Jesus!*' Gently picking her up, he carried her into the bathroom and sat her on the edge of the tub. Blood made everything look worse than it was. But it was still enough to make him realize he could have lost her.

'Goddammit, woman, you could've

killed yourself!' Grabbing a towel, he wet it and put it over the wound. 'Keep that pressed against you while I throw some clothes on and get you fixed up.'

★ ★ ★

Afterward, in the living room, with her wound dressed and both of them in bathrobes on the couch drinking twenty-year-old cognac, the whole incident seemed almost surreal.

'I feel like such an idiot,' she said. 'Oh Mitch, darling, I'm so sorry. I don't know what got into me.'

'Forget it. You're okay, that's all that matters.' He was still pissed, but at himself now more than her, because he realized that after all these years he hadn't learned a damn thing: he'd blindly let himself get sucked in, become emotionally involved with a woman who was out of his class and way too goddamn beautiful and rich for any normal guy to expect to be his; worse, at the same time knowing she was somehow mixed up in the death of his partner. Knowing all this and yet, even as blamed himself for being stupid, needing only to look at her now, all buttery blonde and blue-eyed, cuddled so desirably soft and vulnerable against him, feeling his resistance and common sense melting away; hearing himself saying in a voice so tender he didn't recognize it:

'Feel better now, kitten?'

'Uh-huh . . . ' She ran her tongue over her lips and got a wild look in her eyes. 'Ever had a sexual fantasy?'

'Who hasn't? Wait a minute,' he said as it sank in. 'You tellin' me that shootin' yourself was . . . ?'

Her silence answered his question.

'Jesus,' he said incredulously.

'It's bizarre, I know. And I don't know why it turns me on. Maybe it's the thrill of holding something that can kill you and at the same time thinking about making love to you, I don't know. I just know the two combined — well, it's the ultimate high.'

Mitch didn't know what to say.

Claire saw his expression and gave a disparaging laugh.

'Hard to believe, eh? A rich beautiful chick like me, someone who looks like she's got her act together. Just goes to show you. Nobody's what they seem.' She laughed again, an ugly contemptuous sound. 'And I said Edgar was depraved. Christ, where does that leave me?'

'Everybody has fantasies,' Mitch said lamely. 'Doesn't mean you're depraved.'

'Of course not,' she mocked. 'I mean every ex-Rose Bow! queen dreams of shooting herself while having sex. It's standard procedure. Part of the committee rules. In fact, I think I'll recommend it as the theme for the next Rose Parade.' Her voice was full of self-loathing and suddenly she lost it and burst into tears.

Mitch gently stroked her hair. 'Beatin' yourself up won't help. We are who we are, for better or worse.' Again he sounded lame and he cursed himself for his inability to comfort someone he cared about.

Claire said distantly: 'That's why I'm so protective of Elaina and hate it when people call her crazy. Because if she's crazy it means I might be crazy, too.'

'Knock it off, kitten. You're not crazy

and we both know it. Now, pull yourself together. Ride it out. Come mornin', it won't seem so ugly or hard to deal with.'

She clung to him, trembling. 'Don't leave me, darling, whatever you do. I can't be alone right now.'

'I'm not goin' anywhere.'

'I need you, Mitch. I never thought I'd say that — to anyone. But just being around you, I feel safe and secure for the first time in I don't know how long.'

'You really mean that?'

'With all my heart.'

Mitch kissed her. She stopped trembling. He began to say how great she made him feel but she pressed a finger over his lips and shook her head, silencing him.

'Just hold me, darling. Hold me so tight it hurts.'

He did. They sat there, warm and comfortable in each other's arms, until the dawn broke. Claire was asleep by then and Mitch watched the sun come up. It turned the sky the color of blood.

Red sky at night, shepherd's delight, he thought. Red sky in the morning, shepherd's warning.

16

The next thing Mitch remembered was waking up and realizing he was alone on the couch with a blanket pulled over him. His wrist-watch showed 8:31. He knew he must have dozed off. He yawned and looked around for Claire.

A note on the polished burl coffee table caught his attention. Picking it up, he read: 'Gone to store for eggs. Back in a jiffy. Love you 'off-the-Richter-scale,' Claire.'

Mitch grinned. Tucking the note away, he plodded into the bathroom to take a shower.

It was almost nine when he entered the kitchen. Coffee was perking. Silently blessing an automated world, he poured himself a cup and drank it at the sink while gazing out at the view. The weather had cleared up. The sky was as blue as Claire's eyes. A pale, wafer-like sun looked lonely among the scattered clouds.

It was glaringly bright but had little warmth, its wintry rays yellowing the tops of the pines and, far below, the surface of the lake. Mitch, my man, he told himself, you could get used to this real fast. Oh, yeah. *Real* fast. He chuckled wryly. Dream on, pal . . .

Claire still hadn't returned by ten. Mitch, mildly worried, threw on his jacket and hiked up the trail to the highway. A hundred yards ahead on his left was the convenience store. He walked toward it. A blue Ford pickup truck and a red Jeep Wagoneer were parked out front. As he got closer, the Ford drove away and now he saw there was a third vehicle parked behind the Jeep. It was the black Lincoln Town car. An uneasy feeling chewed at Mitch, making him walk faster.

Inside, the store smelled of fresh-brewed coffee. Mitch looked around. There were two customers, locals who like Mitch had hiked up. But no Claire. Mitch waited for the old gray-bearded storekeeper to ring up both sales, and approached the counter.

'Yessir, what can I do for you?'

'The woman who belongs to the Lincoln outside — know where she is?'

The storekeeper sized Mitch up suspiciously. 'You some kind of cop?'

'Friend. We're stayin' at Grogans' cottage down near the lake. Said she was comin' here for eggs, over an hour ago.'

The storekeeper tucked his plaid wool shirt into his jeans and snapped his red suspenders. 'Don't know nothing 'bout any Grogans owning a cottage 'round here, but the woman — a good-looker about thirty? — she bought eggs, all right. Yessir. Whole dozen. Had me grind her some vanilla nut, too. Like fresh ground coffee, do you, son? I got me all kinds of different varieties — '

'Pop — the woman? Where'd she go?'

'No need to shout, friend, I ain't deef, as they say.'

'Sorry. It's important I know where she went.'

'Wherever it was, it wasn't her choosin'.'

'What d'you mean?'

'Two big-city dinks in a gray limo, longer'n this store, I bet, drove up just as she was leaving. She acted like she didn't wanna go with 'em, but the men pushed her into the back seat and drove off.'

Mitch's heart dropped. 'How long ago?'

'Not sure exactly. Hour maybe less, I dunno, you get my age and time don't seem important. Sure you don't want no fresh ground coffee,' he said as Mitch turned away. 'It's on sale . . . '

The door banged as Mitch ran out.

The storekeeper man snapped his suspenders and scratched his beard. 'City folks, always in such an all-fired hurry to get somewhere ain't important anyway . . . '

Outside, Mitch peered in the driver's side window of the Lincoln. A grocery bag containing a carton of eggs and a bag of coffee sat on the passenger seat; also a greeting card and a car-rental contract weighted down with a cellular phone. Mitch tried the doors. Locked! He picked up a rock and broke the passenger-side window. Instantly, the alarm went off. Mitch reached in and grabbed the card and rental contract, ran across the highway and down the slope into the trees.

He ran through the pines for as long as

his breath held out. Then, winded, he sat on a stump and looked at the rental contract. It was signed by Claire Dixon and listed her address in San Marino, California. Well, at least that tied in with what she'd told him. He put the contract in his pocket and looked at the envelope. His name was penciled on it. He took out the card. On the front a cute, sexy schoolgirl in a tight mini-skirt was being chased by an old lecherous professor whose fly was open. Inside, the caption read: 'Slow down, Rita! I just wanna carry your books!' Below, Claire had scribbled a brief rhyme:

'When we get back to L.A.,
You can carry *this* schoolgirl's books
Every day!'

Mitch smiled and tucked the card away.

* * *

He searched the cottage thoroughly. He did not find anything significant until he came across a flat metal box in a drawer under the kitchen counter. In it was correspondence from various business associates, all addressed to Mr. Edgar Bennett either at his estate in San Marino or at the cottage. Also, a leather folder containing stationery with gold embossed Edgar V. Bennett and BENCO INDUSTRIES letterheads.

A cold feeling hit Mitch as he realized Claire had lied to him. But, why? What difference did it make if the cottage belonged to someone named Grogan or Edgar Bennett? Had she thought that if he knew it was owned by her stepfather it might have affected the way he felt about her? It would be pretty to think so, but Mitch doubted it. The world he lived in was seldom pretty and he had no reason to believe it was going to change now.

But he was not a man who rushed to judgment. Returning the box to the drawer, he made sure the place did not look like it had been ransacked, and then called the sheriff's office. When Sheriff Briggs came on the line, Mitch asked him if he'd heard anything new.

'That little matter concerning the CHP,' the sheriff said guardedly. 'The leak didn't come from there.'

'Where, then?'

'Good question. Which channel did you say you heard it on?'

'I didn't,' Mitch said. 'Someone told me about it and I never asked 'em which channel.'

'Well, it wasn't one of the local ones. I called around and none of their newscasters mentioned it.'

'Interesting,' Mitch said. Pieces of the puzzle were beginning to fit together in his mind and he now knew exactly where he had to go next. 'I'll be in touch, Sheriff.' Hanging up, he looked out the window, over the tops of the pines, at the wintry blue lake, thinking: Sure would be nice if a guy knew which direction Samarra was . . .

17

The drive from Lake Tahoe to Reseda took Mitch almost seven hours. Traffic wasn't bad until he reached the Valley, then everything became a slow crawl. Darkness settled in.

Famished, Mitch stopped at an IHOP. It was crowded but he found a table that did not stick to his elbows and wolfed down a stack of blueberry pancakes smothered in syrup and a side order of link sausages. He washed it all down with black coffee, knowing he had a long night ahead of him and needed to be alert.

He then drove to Willow Street, where he lived, and parked outside the home of one of the local bikers. Lights showed inside the rundown clapboard house and heavy metal rock blared into the night. Mitch opened the gate and made his way between three chopped Harleys parked haphazardly on the dirt lawn. A snarling Pit Bull charged out from under the front porch and hurled itself at Mitch. He didn't move. The dog got within a foot of him before being yanked off its feet by its chain.

'Knock it off, Heinie,' Mitch told the frothing dog, ''fore you choke yourself to death.' He stepped onto the rickety porch and banged on the front door. Boots clunked on the other side of the door but it didn't open.

'Yeah?'

'It's me, Hawk, Mitch Holliday — open up.'

Locks rasped open. The door swung inward to reveal Henry 'Hawk' Huckle, a huge biker of fifty with a scraggly red beard, sagging beer belly and greasy Levi's held up by a chrome crankshaft chain. He was a mass of tattoos and happily stoned. He grinned lopsidedly and thrust his big, oily paw out to Mitch.

'Hey, Big Daddy, what's up?'

'Same old, same old,' Mitch said. A sickly sweet smell drifted toward him and over Hawk's shoulder he could see a bunch of bikers dismantling a Harley in the living room. 'Sorry to bug you, but I need a favor.'

'You got it, man.'

'I want to talk to Conan for a few minutes.'

'Sure, man. Shut up!' he yelled to the snarling Pit Bull. Then, as the dog slunk back under the porch: 'He's out back pissin' around in his office.' He chuckled and scratched his bald head. 'Weird, ain't it? I used to think kids were nothin' but a fuckin' nuisance, but now, hell, I don't know what I'd do without the little bastard.'

'Times they are a-changing,' Mitch said congenially.

'Amen, brother. Need a hit?' he added, jerking his thumb toward the living room. 'It's good shit.'

'Thanks, but I got a full night ahead of me.' Mitch left the porch and headed back along the driveway to the garage. The door was closed but a sliver of light showed along the bottom. Inside, Eminem was rapping. Mitch walked around to a side door and banged on it. A key turned and a tall, dark-haired boy of thirteen peered out. He wore a Harley Davidson T-shirt, baggy jeans, and sneakers with the laces untied. A snake tattoo crawled up his forearm and three gold rings were stapled in his left ear. He grinned as he saw Mitch.

'Hi, Mr. Holliday,' he said, and held the door open so Mitch could enter. 'Shoot anybody lately?'

'Just a couple of snotty teenagers — nothin' to write home about.'

Conan laughed. 'You've been talkin' to my old man again.' He led Mitch to his desk, a white plastic job that was jammed in the corner among stacks of newly chromed exhaust pipes. The rest of the garage was filled to the ceiling with spare motorcycle parts, all neatly arranged on shelves and hooks and in bins along the walls.

Conan sat at the desk and turned down the volume on the twin speakers flanking his laptop.

'Who you want me to look up this time?' he asked.

'Just a guy I might be doin' business with. If you got time?'

'Sure thing. I'm almost finished with this, anyway.' He scrolled down the columns of Harley Davidson parts listed on the screen. 'What d'you think?' he said, indicating the screen. 'Pretty cool, huh?'

'What is it?'

'A catalogue of all the spare parts my dad's got for sale.'

'Very impressive.'

'See, this way he don't never have to worry if he's selling stuff back to guys he rip — well, you know. Where he got 'em from.'

'Sounds like a winner to me,' Mitch said. He watched as Conan saved the material and then punched up his Google search program.

'Okay, Mr. H, what's this dude's name?'

'Bennett,' Mitch said. 'Edgar Bennett. Middle initial 'V' for Vincent. I want to know all about him.'

18

Twenty minutes later Mitch drove the rented Dodge compact into his driveway. Killing the lights he sat there, parked, with the engine still running, trying to decide if he should tell Donna about Lionel now or wait until after he returned from San Marino. Ahead, through the old chain-link gate, he could see lights shining in Lionel's house on the adjoining lot.

Lionel had bought the three-bedroom tract home nine years ago, six months after he married Donna Capetti, a waitress of Sicilian descent who worked graveyard at Denny's. As he told Mitch, it was not his dream house but it was all he could afford, even with a vet loan, and it did have a fenced lot with walnut trees, oleander, and room to build a pool if he ever hit it big. It was also in a white neighborhood, which was important to Lionel, even though some of the whites around him were leftover Hell's Angels who threw wild marijuana parties, drank cheap wine, and fired up their 'hogs' day or night. But they did not give him or Donna any trouble and, in a way, Lionel was pleased to have them around, because just looking at them made him feel superior.

He had married Donna because she was white, too, and became angry when she referred to herself as 'Sicilian swarthy.' He also liked it that she was Denny's most popular waitress and was built exactly how Lionel liked his women: full-lipped and big-breasted with a seductive, defiant look that gave him a hard-on every time he saw her. Lionel didn't know squat about Sicilian women. But he did know Donna was hot and he felt great with her on his arm, knowing that most guys would have given up a case of Bud or even Super Bowl tickets just to have her in his bed.

For anyone who knew Lionel well, like Mitch, it all made sense. What did not make sense was why Donna had married a loser like Lionel. 'Because I flat-out loved him,' she said when Mitch first asked her. 'Is that so hard to believe? Okay,' she said when he didn't answer. 'So love lasted all of an hour and a half. How was I supposed to know he'd turn into a mean-assed punk who cheats on me all the time?' Anyway, she went on, it didn't matter because by then she'd gained what she'd wanted all along: two wonderful, smart, healthy kids who made up for everything.

Thinking about that now, Mitch heard children's laughter coming from the shingle-roofed house and decided right then and there not to tell Donna about Lionel's death until tomorrow morning. Bad news, he justified to himself, was always better when ingested by daylight.

Gently pushing open the gate with the bumper, he pulled up beside his unfinished, cement-hulled sailboat. The 38-foot boat (named *Ugly Momma* by the bikers) had no mast, was supported by scaffolding and the only way to board it was by a stepladder leaned against the starboard side. Parked nearby were two cars: a beat-up '82 T-bird that ran well and, under a tarp covered by dust and leaves, the love of his life: a vintage two-tone orange-and-white '54 Starfire Oldsmobile convertible with matching upholstery and spinner hub-caps. Mitch had bought it as a pile of junk ten years ago, when he'd been in the chips as a private investigator, and lovingly restored it. It had taken twenty thousand dollars and six years to return the car to show-room condition, which said something about Mitch's patience; and now that it was 'cherry' (as his dad would've said) he only drove it on Sundays, and then only if the weather was good. As a result, the rebuilt Rocket V-8 engine still had less than three thousand miles on it.

Mitch quietly climbed aboard the sail-boat and went below. Leaving the lights off so as not to alert Donna, he took a quick shower, put on a black sweater and blue jeans, and collected a zippered gym bag that already held what he called his 'work tools.'

It was not easy finding everything in the dark, but he was back outside in less than fifteen minutes and about to put the bag into the trunk when he heard Donna's footsteps crunching on the gravel driveway. *Damn*, he thought. *Now he'd have to tell her about Lionel.* He turned, not seeing her at first in the dark; and then squinting as her flashlight shone in his eyes.

'Going somewhere?'

'Hi, kiddo — '

'Don't 'kiddo' me, you jerk.' She shone the light on his bag. 'Sneaking out like a fucking thief in the night!'

'I wasn't sneakin' — '

She slapped him. It stung and made his eyes water but he took it without a word. That made her even angrier. She went to slap him again, but this time he grabbed her wrist, saying, 'Whoa, only one to a customer.'

'Let go, damn you.'

'Then cool it. Hear me out.' He waited till she stopped struggling. 'I got bad news, Donna. Lionel's dead.'

'Tell me something I don't know.'

Mitch hid his surprise. 'Did Sheriff Briggs contact you?'

'Yes. Said he traced me through Lionel's guns.'

'And here I thought the only thing he

149

could focus on was his butt.'

'What?'

Mitch, unaware he had voiced his thoughts, said: 'Inside joke.'

'Well, if that isn't just like you. Lionel's dead and you're making stupid jokes!'

'Hey, why you bustin' my balls? I didn't kill him.'

'Then, why'd you pawn his guns?'

'To save carrying 'em around,' he lied.

'That why you also torched his car?'

'No, that was to keep a promise.'

'Fuck you and your lies, Mitch Holliday.'

'I'm not lyin'. Lionel wanted to be cremated, not buried in the ground like some chewed-up dog bone, so I gave him the closest I could to a Viking funeral.'

Donna glared suspiciously at him. 'Lionel never told me anything about being cremated.'

'Baby, there's a ton of things he never told you. And one day, when I got time, I'll be happy to compare notes. Right now, I'm more interested in what else the sheriff told you.'

'Nothing.' She stepped closer, the smell of garlic on her breath, her dark eyes searching Mitch's face for some kind of emotional giveaway that would tell her what she really wanted to know. But it wasn't there.

'Mitch, tell me the truth: did-you-kill-him?'

'Hell, no. Why would I kill Lionel?'

'On account of us, maybe?' She tucked the flashlight into her faded blue robe and put her arms about his neck. 'A woman likes to think a man loves her enough to do anything for her.'

'Sorry to disappoint you.'

'I'll get over it — 'specially now there's nobody to keep us from being together.' She kissed him hungrily; then, disappointed in his response, snapped: 'Is that the best you can do?'

'Donna . . . Lionel knew about us.'

'So?'

'So, I wish he hadn't.'

'Since when'd you grow a conscience?'

'That's not funny. Lionel was a jerk-off in many ways, but a guy could do worse for a partner.'

Men, she thought. If she lived to be a hundred, she'd never understand them. But they were the only game in town and she wanted this one, regardless.

'Okay, so Lionel knew about us and I knew about him. That makes us even.'

'Maybe, but it doesn't make me feel less guilty.'

'So, get over it. I did.' She headed back to the house.

'If anyone asks,' Mitch told her, 'you haven't seen me.'

'Why should I lie for you?'

''Cause I'm supposed to be in Tahoe and because, when this is over, I'll see to it you and the kids are taken care of.'

'You say that now, when I'm about to cut your cajones off, but how do I know you won't run out on me later?'

Mitch grinned and looked about him. 'What, an' give up all this luxury?'

Donna was not amused. 'You better not be jerking me around,' she warned, 'or you'll wind up looking for it in the grass, like that Bobbit guy.'

'You should write for Hallmark,' Mitch told her. He slammed the trunk and got into the car. Donna watched him drive off, hoping she had not pushed him too far, and then returned inside the house.

19

The tail end of rush hour traffic was still clogging the freeways and it took Mitch over an hour to reach the Bennett estate in exclusive San Marino. It was a huge place with a terraced swimming pool, tennis court and manicured grounds surrounded by ivy-covered walls.

Thanks to the detailed profile of Edgar Bennett that Conan had pulled off the Internet, Mitch knew almost everything about the man and the people who'd come in contact with him. That included Mrs. Constance Winslow, a reclusive widow whom Frank Lloyd Wright had built the mansion for in 1921. Mrs. Winslow came from 'Old Pasadena Money' and after her husband died of leukemia in '24, she had never left the estate. Nothing else was known about her except that she always wore gray, loved animals, and was occasionally seen walking the grounds with two leashed ocelots. There had once even been peacocks. But their shrill human-like cries upset the neighbors and long before the oil-rich Dixons from Oklahoma bought the place in '74, the last bird had 'mysteriously' died and Sarah Dixon, the mother of Claire and Elaina, had been too busy caring for her stroke-ridden husband to worry about replacing a 'bunch of noisy birds.'

But in '86, when 'Papa Emmit' finally obliged everyone by dying, Sarah told her daughters that she'd had a vision in which all of Mrs. Winslow's peacocks came to her and said they had been poisoned to death by the gardener, a shriveled up old Japanese man whom Sarah 'just knew' had been bribed by their next-door neighbors, the Carmichaels. No one believed her. But it did say something about Sarah's state of mind and laid the groundwork for all the gossip that sprang up when she married Edgar Bennett, a hustling lawyer, many years her junior, whom she met at the country club and married almost before the echoes of the gravediggers' shovels faded from the cemetery.

Sarah, the neighbors agreed, was off her rocker and no one was surprised when she died in a boating accident on Lake Tahoe. Nor were they surprised when Edgar Bennett inherited all the money. They had expected that. But they *were* surprised that he did not have his youngest stepdaughter committed. Her constant suicide attempts, irrational outbursts in public and efforts to seduce everything that entered the grounds were notorious. But, to the neighbors' disgust, Edgar Bennett chose to hire armed bodyguards, install security cameras and string razor-wire along the top of the ivy-covered walls, making the grand old estate look like a damned mental hospital.

Now, as Mitch drove past the electric gates, he could see the lighted grounds and, up near the mansion, Mace walking a Doberman. Mitch drove around behind the estate and parked near the chauffeur's quarters. Donning leather gloves, he climbed onto the hood and pulled himself up on the wall. Straddling the razor-wire, he took out a pocket alarm-detector and aimed it down at the ground. It illuminated the laser beams that criss-crossed through the shrubbery below. Mitch picked a grassy spot to land and jumped off. He hit hard, stumbled, and went sprawling. As he lay there a moment, winded, he heard a rustling noise beside him.

It was the Doberman he had seen with Mace. It charged out of the bushes, stood over him and thrust its jaws in his face. Mitch smelled its bad breath.

'Good boy . . . Nice doggie . . . '

The Dobie growled. Mitch slowly reached toward his shoulder-holster.

'I don't suppose you care that this has been a lousy week for me?'

The Dobie watched him, drooling.

'I didn't think so.' Saliva dripped onto Mitch's lips. Sweat ran down his nose. 'See, I know why you guys are so dangerous, being the second fastest dog in the world an' all, but' — he had the gun out of the holster now and was inching it up toward the Dobie — 'this cannon fires a .45 slug and I hope you don't believe that Superman bullshit about bein' faster than a speedin' bullet 'cause then I'd have to shoot you and then one of those dumb morons feeding you'll come runnin' up and tattoo his initials on my chest with his Uzi.'

The Dobie did not move. Mitch took a chance and slowly got up. The Dobie watched him, motionless.

'Wish I could figure out what your story is before I need stitches,' Mitch said. Walking now, 'I mean, is there some invisible line out here that when I cross it you rip my nuts off?' Walking faster now, the Dobie trotting abreast of him, fangs bared.

Mitch, unnerved, said, 'Fuck it,' and took off running.

The Dobie loped along beside him.

The two made it across the lawn, around the swimming pool, up the steps to the lighted terrace and on, until they reached the French doors of the study. Mitch stopped to catch his breath. The Dobie also stopped, content to copy the man's every movement.

Mitch tried the doorknob. The door opened. 'Here's where I leave you, pal,' and he ducked inside. The Dobie urinated on a planter, sat down on its own shadow and waited for Mitch to reappear.

It was dark in the study. Mitch moved quietly across the room and peered out the door into the hallway. Lit by the portico light, it led to a marble foyer that wouldn't have shamed the Getty museum.

Mitch crept to the foyer without seeing anyone. Jazz music was playing in one of the rooms off the landing at the top of the stairway. Mitch started up the stairs, suddenly stopping as in the dim light he saw someone sitting halfway up. It was Elaina, in lemon lounging pajamas that accentuated her flaming-red hair, drinking from a near-empty bottle of vodka. If she saw Mitch, frozen six stairs below her, she showed no sign of it; instead, she seemed confused by the fact that she couldn't drink from the bottle and suck her thumb at the same time.

Mitch cleared his throat, and as she turned her boozy green eyes toward him, said in his visiting uncle's voice: 'You must be Elaina.'

'Uh-uh. Tinkerbelle.'

'Of course,' he said. 'Why didn't I think of that?'

'Who are you?'

'A friend of your sister's. Seen her around?'

'No.' She giggled and sucked her thumb. 'I really am Tinkerbelle, you know . . . ' Dropping the bottle, she pulled herself up by the banister. 'See . . . I can fly.'

She half-leaped, half-fell toward Mitch who had no choice but to dive forward and catch her.

'My savior . . . ' She tried to kiss him, but he turned his head. 'Did you ride in on a white horse?'

'Hundred'n twenty horses, courtesy of Dodge.'

Elaina giggled and sucked her thumb. 'You're cute, you know that.'

'Does that mean you'll tell me where Claire is?'

She said: 'Want to feel what Jesus gave me?' Taking his thumb, she guided it into her mouth, pressing it up into the hollow ridge and working it around so he would feel the sensation. 'Feel that? It's what makes me so special, guys say.'

'I'll bet.' Mitch retrieved his wet thumb.

'Carry me up to my bedroom and I'll let you find out for yourself.'

'He's gonna be too busy for that,' said a voice below. A light clicked on downstairs. Mitch saw Taggert and Mace standing in a doorway leading off the foyer, their Uzis aimed at him. 'Put her down, fella.'

Mitch gently set Elaina down. She pulled on his collar until his ear met her lips, said in a stage whisper: 'I think they wuz expecting you, Holden.'

'Shut up,' Taggert told her. He waggled his Uzi at Mitch. 'Get down here and keep your hands where we can see 'em.'

'Put your guns away.' Claire leaned over the upstairs banister. Her hair hung loosely about the shoulders of her revealing nightgown and she still held the initialed silver hairbrush she'd been using. 'Let Mr. Holliday go.'

'But he broke in.'

'I don't care what he did. Let him go. That's an order, Taggert.'

'We don't take orders from you, only

Mr. Bennett. And his orders were to shoot anyone who breaks in.'

There was a tense beat as no-one moved. Mitch, tired of their bull, decided to make it easy for them.

'Who the hell you people tryin' to kid? Nobody's gonna shoot me. So, why don't you quit your stupid little game 'fore I get pissed and shove those Uzis up your two sorry asses.'

'Watch your mouth — ' Taggert began.

'Or what?' said Mitch. 'Tell 'em,' he said to Claire. 'You went to a lot of trouble to get me here and here I am. But I've taken all the crap I'm gonna take, so either blow off this fake dog-and-pony show or I'm takin' a hike.'

Elaina giggled. 'Sooo cute. Isn't he cute, sis?'

Claire knew the game was over and didn't want her sister involved in what was coming next. 'Sweetie, go up to your room, okay?'

'What, and miss all the fun?'

'Do as I say, please. Help her,' Claire said to Taggert. Then, beckoning to Mitch: 'Come on up . . . '

20

Mitch followed Claire into her bedroom. He had been in smaller bowling alleys. And all of them had cost less to decorate. Priceless antique furniture, original oils by Monet, Cezanne and Degas, and a four poster bed big enough to sail across the Pacific. Mitch could not imagine what it all added up to. Hell, the cost of the snowy, deep-piled carpet alone would have fed Ethiopia for a year.

Claire gestured to the brocaded Queen Anne loveseat and told him to get comfortable. He sat gingerly, afraid his weight might collapse its fragile legs.

'Cognac okay?' She did not wait for his answer but went to the wet bar and poured two snifters half-full of fifty-year-old brandy.

'You don't believe in cheatin' yourself, do you?' Mitch said, looking about him.

Claire handed him his cognac, sat beside him and swirled her drink around in the snifter before answering, 'Would you?'

'Not if I had your money.' He took a sip, felt the amber fluid melt down his throat and a warm glow start in his stomach. 'Which brings me to the million dollar question: why mess with me?'

'I find you attractive.'

Mitch set his glass down and stood up.

'Where're you going?'

'Home.'

'I've offended you?'

'People who think I'm stupid always offend me.'

'Calling you attractive makes you stupid?'

'Only if I believed you,' Mitch growled. 'Look,' he continued, 'maybe I didn't make myself clear on the stairs back down there. Or maybe that ditzy little nympho sister of yours has all the family brains. Either way, I came here to find out the truth and unless you quit lyin' and tell me what the hell's goin' on, I'm leaving. And this time, lady, all the sex, phony rapes and fake kidnappings in the world won't bring me back!'

Claire arched her eyebrows. 'My God, for a guy who is so laid-back you really get steamed up, don't you?'

'Only when my buttons are pushed.'

'And I'm pushing them?'

'With both fists.'

'Interesting.' She sipped her cognac, holding the snifter with both hands and eyeing him over the rim of the glass as if contemplating how to deal with him. 'Very well, then I'll stop pushing them.'

Silence. Mitch remained standing.

'Sit down, for God's sake, will you?' When he didn't, she said: 'Please.'

He sat. Claire took another sip of cognac, closed her eyes as if trying to visualize not only what she was about to say but what kind of repercussions to expect, then said calmly:

'You're right, Mr. Holliday, I have lied to you. A lot. And my hard-to-get routine, the rape attempt in the parking lot and my disappearing act outside the store by the lake were all fake, just as you say. Fake — but necessary.'

'Why?'

'At first, because you were my only link

to Lionel. Then, once you had me hooked, I had to make sure you wanted more than a one-night stand; that you cared enough for me to track me down, regardless of whether I was lying or not. No,' she said as he started to speak, 'let me finish. Having said all that, I want to make something very clear — what happened between us in the cottage — that wasn't faked. That was all as real as it gets and it's never happened to me before. You must believe that.'

'Why-he-asked?'

'Because I love you. Go ahead, raise your eyebrows, roll your eyes, sneer, do whatever it is that you do when you think you're being conned. I don't care. None of it's important. What is important, the *only* thing that's important is that I love you and I want you to love me. I also want you to trust me. Oh, I know I don't deserve your trust,' she said as he looked amused, 'and I wouldn't blame you one bit if you threw your brandy in my face, told me to go hump myself and walked out.'

'Yes, you would. You'd be really pissed.'

She laughed. 'You're right. I would. But you know what I mean.'

'I'd like to think I do.'

'Then do as I ask and believe me. What're you thinking?' she added when he didn't say anything.

'Lies on top of lies on top of lies.'

'Only I'm not lying, Mitch. And I can prove it.'

'Then start with why Lionel Banks set me up. Then tell me what he meant to you and why two dumb junkies like Lila Hendricks and Joey-what's-his-face died for a cigar box full of fake ice.'

'Fake ice?' Her eyes popped open. 'What do you mean?'

'The diamonds — they were paste.'

'Never.'

'Ask Sheriff Briggs if you think I'm lying. He's the one who told me.'

'B-But that's impossible. They were Elaina's.'

Mitch stared at her, thinking she was either telling the truth or the greatest liar he'd ever met. 'Then someone must've switched 'em.'

'Like, who?'

'I don't know. Maybe Lionel — '

'My God,' Claire exclaimed. 'If that's true, it means he intended to kill Lila and Joey right from the start — ' She broke off, as if she'd said too much.

'Don't bother puttin' on the brakes, kitten, not unless you want to see this horse leavin' the corral.'

'No,' she said bravely. 'I said I'd tell you the truth and I will, no matter what.' She sipped her cognac, eyes clouding over for a few moments as she tried to sort out what she wanted to say. Finally, she said: 'It all started about two years ago. Elaina had begun to walk again with the help of crutches and needed someone to drive her around. I persuaded Edgar to call an agency for a chauffeur and the next day, Lionel showed up. Stop me if you know all this — '

'You're doin' fine,' Mitch said. 'Go on.'

'Everything went great for a few months, then Edgar caught Elaina in bed with Lionel.'

'Big surprise.'

'It was, back then. Elaina's always been on a different runway than the rest of us,

167

but she didn't always play musical beds. Before the accident and mother's death, and for a brief period right after, she was pretty fussy about whose bed she put her shoes under.'

'Keep goin'.'

'Well, Edgar had a cow. He had Taggert and Mace beat the crap out of Lionel and then fired him.'

'Sounds reasonable.'

'Except that Elaina wasn't just screwing Lionel to piss off Edgar, like she normally does — she actually loved him. Or thought she did.'

'Didn't she know Lionel was married?'

'He promised to dump his wife and run off with her. I know,' she said as Mitch raised his eyebrows, 'I didn't believe him either. But Elaina did and, more importantly, so did Edgar — enough to threaten to have Lionel killed and her committed if she didn't break it off.'

'All the makings of a daytime Soap. But where do I fit in? Hell, I didn't even know Lionel back then.'

'Cut to two months ago. Elaina, who all along had been sneaking out to see Lionel

— she was buying Mace and Taggert's silence by screwing them, in case you're wondering — offered him a million dollars to do away with Edgar.'

'How would little sister get her hands on that kind of dough?'

'She told Lionel she'd cash in some stocks. All she needed was a little time, so Edgar wouldn't get suspicious — '

'And meanwhile she gave him her jewels as collateral?'

Claire nodded. 'They're worth at least a million and Lionel jumped at the offer. But in order to kill someone you have to know their exact timetable and where-abouts. And since Edgar moves around more often than Bin Laden, Lionel figured he needed someone reliable, someone he could trust.'

'Like your ex-maid, Lila Hendricks?'

Claire smiled. 'You've done your homework, I see.'

'Just tryin' to keep abreast of things. Go on.'

'Lionel was doing her between washing our cars and 'Driving Miss Daisy,' and once he'd hooked Lila with sex, he promised to cut her and Joey in, if they'd help him take down Edgar.'

'How come he needed them when he had Elaina? Surely she knew when and where her stepfather was most of the time?'

'I just told you: she's not reliable.'

'And two junkies are?'

'Only one — Lila was recreational then.'

'Still not a good risk for a guy with Lionel's nature.'

'Better than Elaina. She's my baby sister and I'd do anything for her. But you've seen her — she's wiggy, and Lionel wasn't about to trust her with his neck.'

'Or yours.'

'I wasn't involved. Not then. I *wasn't*,' she said as he looked doubtful. 'That's the God's honest truth.'

'Okay, we'll table that for now. You still haven't said where I come in.'

'You can't kill an Edgar Bennett without creating your worst police nightmare. Despite all their political yin-yang about serving the little people, what the cops are really paid for is to protect the rich and they take it very personally when one of their darling VIPs dies, tearing down heaven and hell to find the killer. Lionel knew this and decided he needed — '

'A fall guy!' Mitch said as it hit him. 'Jesus, that's what he meant.'

'Meant?'

'Just before Lionel croaked, he tried to tell me that he'd set me up. But why, dammit? We were partners and — Sonofabitch,' he said, suddenly realizing. 'Donna!'

'Lionel's wife? What about her?'

'We slept together once and Lionel, he found out about it.' Mitch shook his head. 'What goes around, comes around.'

'And always when you least expect it. What?' she said as he frowned. 'What'd you just think of?'

'I was just wondering. When fate took Lionel out of the mix, why'd you pick me? And don't give me that crap again about how attractive I am.'

'You are, in a rough-and-tumble sort of way. But no, that wasn't the reason. When Lionel didn't show, and I realized something had gone wrong, Elaina came unglued and spilled her guts to me.'

'And you, noble and protective sister that you are, rushed to her help, right?'

'Save your sarcasm. When it comes to Elaina, I make no excuses. I'm all she has.'

Mitch let it go, saying: 'Okay, so you needed a replacement fast. That still doesn't nominate me, a guy you knew nothin' about.'

'I knew enough. Lionel had told Elaina about your money laundering bust and he said he'd already asked you to help him nail Lila — '

'Which, of course, he never intended to do.'

'Truthfully, I don't know what he intended to do. I asked him, but he said the less I knew the better off I'd be should something go wrong — which at the time I thought was rather noble of him.'

'There had to be more to it than that. Lionel wouldn't know noble if it climbed up and chewed him a new asshole.'

'I'm sure you're right. But whatever his reason, it had to connect you in some way to Edgar, so the police would believe that you'd killed him. Though he wouldn't have needed much if he'd known it was going to be all over the news that you'd shot Joey in the motel while screwing Lila — '

'Not exactly a poster boy image, huh?'

'Let's say it seemed 'safe' to assume that you'd go along.'

'What's sex got to do with morality, right?'

They both laughed and sipped their cognac, minds churning, expressions hiding what they were really thinking.

'So, now you know everything,' Claire said.

'Not everything. You still haven't explained why your sister's jewelry was fake.'

'You just said — Lionel must've switched them.'

'And if he didn't?'

'I wouldn't have the vaguest idea.'

'How about Babycakes? She could've sold 'em off, little by little, and had fakes made.'

'Elaina's not that smart. She has

trouble remembering the last guy she slept with. No, it has to be Lionel, Lila, or Joey. And my money's on Lionel. He was supposed to return the jewelry once we — Elaina gave him the million dollars. He must have decided to make a little extra on the side.'

'It's not impossible,' Mitch said, ignoring her slip. 'He knew you guys couldn't blow the whistle on him without incriminating yourselves. It was the perfect setup.'

Claire chewed silently on her lower lip.

'Okay, so we've pretty much figured out what happened to the jewels. Tell me what goes down next. You didn't mark a trail for me to follow just 'cause I'm sexy or attractive. You must still think I'll whack Edgar for the right price. Correct?'

'I'd be lying if I said 'no,' and I did promise not to lie anymore.'

'So you did.'

'Interested?'

'Maybe. I'd have to think about it. When is our next window of opportunity?'

'Two days — when Edgar returns from

174

a bankers' summit in the Bahamas. He's flying in late Friday night, will be here all through Saturday and then, Sunday morning early, he's off to the land of cuckoo clocks and Pinocchio.'

'So, basically, we're lookin' at twenty-four hours.' Mitch shrugged. 'That's time enough to whack anybody.'

'I hope so. To keep Edgar from committing Elaina, I've promised to marry him.'

'When?'

'No date. But he'll be after me the minute he returns, so we don't have forever.'

Mitch finished his cognac, mulling it over very carefully before saying: 'If — I repeat, *if* — I do this, I call all the shots and only you and I are involved.'

'Absolutely. And Mitch,' the smell of wet lilacs mingled with the cognac fragrance flooded his senses as she leaned close, 'I don't expect you to do this alone. Much as I hate violence, I'll help any way I can.' She kissed him. Halfway through the kiss, Mitch pulled away and stood up.

'I gotta go.'

'You're not staying the night?'

'I think better when I sleep alone.'

'Sleeping wasn't exactly what I had in mind.'

'That's why I'm goin'.' He moved to the door, turned and grinned at her. 'But, hold that thought.' He left, leaving Claire looking thoughtfully after him. Mitch descended the stairs and crossed to the front door. A vase of long-stemmed roses caught his eye. Deciding they might put him in good with Donna, he grabbed them and hurried out.

Outside, the moon had gone behind the clouds and it smelled like rain. Mitch pulled his gloves on and hurried around back to the pool area. Not wanting anyone to see him with the roses, he headed for the back gate. Almost there, he heard a growl to his right and the Dobie stepped out of the shrubbery. It was all teeth and snarls.

'What's your problem? I thought we were buddies?'

The Dobie growled menacingly.

'I guess not.' Mitch looked at the gate, knew the Dobie would nail him before he could unbolt it, and decided upon the wall. The Dobie inched toward him, fangs bared. Mitch knew he was a dead cigar but was about to run for it anyway, when Claire called to him from her balcony.

'Mitch — '

'I'm a little busy right now — '

'Drop the roses.'

'What?'

'The roses! Get rid of them!' She indicated the Dobie. 'He's trained to let anybody in, but nobody out if they're carrying something.'

As Claire got to the word 'something' the Dobie sprang at Mitch. He hurled the roses in the dog's face and sprinted for the wall. He made it there just ahead of the snarling Dobie. Leaping, he grabbed a handful of ivy and pulled himself up. He felt the dog's teeth graze his leg, heard cloth ripping and then he was astride the wall, his gloves saving his hands from being ripped by the razor-wire.

Mitch looked back at Claire, who stood laughing on the balcony.

'What's so funny?'

'You. Should've seen yourself scrambling up that wall.'

'Monkey see, monkey do,' he said, grinning.

'Serves you right,' she said. 'Next time, cheapskate, buy the roses.' She blew him a kiss and went back inside.

Mitch looked down at the Dobie. It was on its hind-legs, paws against the wall, snapping at Mitch's trailing leg. Mitch gave it the finger and leaped off the wall on the other side.

21

Driving the Dodge compact to the nearest Avis office in the Valley, Mitch turned the car back in. One of the kids working there was just getting off work. Mitch offered him five bucks to drive him home. The kid said, Make it ten, mister, and you got a deal. Mitch paid him the tenspot, marveling as he did at how little the dollar bought these days.

Later, when he approached his sailboat, he saw a note taped to the stepladder. It was from Donna and told him to call Sheriff Briggs. Mitch looked at the house. It was late but a light was on and Mitch knew Donna was still up, probably watching TV. He went and banged on the door. Donna opened it, iron in hand. Mitch did not give her a chance to speak, but angrily waved the note in her face.

'Nice to know I can rely on you to keep your word.'

'Fuck you!' Donna slammed the door

in his face and returned to her ironing.

Mitch opened the door, stepped into the living room and watched Donna press a crease in a pair of boy's jeans.

She looked tired. He knew being a single working mother was tough and he respected her for carrying the load without complaining or feeling sorry for herself.

He suddenly felt a growing urge to throw his arms about her and promise to protect her from all her problems — an urge that surprised him because long ago, after he had slept with her that once, he'd woken up the next morning feeling no love for her, just guilt, and despite Donna's efforts to make a big emotional deal out of it, he had resisted all her talk about love and future commitment and left the house thinking it had just been a one-night stand. Now, as he watched her ironing, doubt entered his mind. Maybe he had made a mistake about Donna. Maybe, with Lionel out of the way, he might want to try a relationship with her.

Donna misunderstood his glowering silence. 'I didn't tell the sheriff you were here,' she said, still angry but trying not to start a war, 'because he never asked. Just told me to tell you to call him.'

Mitch realized he had jumped the gun. But he found apologizing difficult, so he turned to leave.

'Better use my phone,' Donna said. 'They turned yours off this afternoon.'

'Guess they weren't kiddin' about paying my bill.'

'I told them to take the Olds in payment, but they didn't seem to think it was a fair deal.'

Mitch chuckled, 'Screw you,' and grabbed the phone.

'Number's on the pad,' she pointed. Mitch punched in the number and, after several rings, Sheriff Briggs came on.

'What's up?' Mitch asked him.

'Thanks for telling me you left town, Holliday.'

'Must've slipped my mind. But that isn't why you called, right?'

'The D.A spoke to me about Joey's shooting. He's settled on self-defense. Seems a briefcase full of fake jewelry ain't the best evidence to hang a murder charge on you.'

'That mean I'm off the hook?'

'For now.'

'Don't sound so disappointed. Under all this shit, I'm basically a good guy.'

'So Donna kept reminding me. You hit paydirt there, soldier.'

'I'm beginnin' to find that out,' Mitch said, watching Donna ironing in front of the TV. 'Anything else?'

'Nope. How about you?'

'Things are so quiet, making me nervous.'

The sheriff laughed. 'I know what you mean. Take her slow, Holliday.'

Mitch hung up and turned to Donna. 'Can I ask you some questions about Lionel without us going to war?'

'I doubt it. Talking of war,' she added, 'what the hell happened to your pants?'

Mitch looked down at his ripped pant-leg as if seeing it for the first time. 'Man, how'd that happen?'

Donna rolled her eyes. 'Pur-lease . . . '

Mitch ignored her sarcasm. 'If Lionel wanted to hide somethin' important, you got any idea where it might be?'

'Like, what important?'

'Like, anything important.'

'Depending on what it is, depends on where he'd hide it.'

Mitch was losing his patience. Donna did that to him. She was one of the few persons who knew how to push his buttons. He said: 'Somethin' the size of a cigar box. Come on, Donna,' he said when she didn't answer. 'Don't make a federal case out of this.'

'I'm thinking, I'm thinking . . . In his car, most likely.'

'Great.'

'That's right, I forgot. You torched his car, didn't you?'

'Piss off.'

'I love a snappy comeback.'

'And I'd love it if you'd just answer my goddamn question. I mean, would he hide it in the garage or — or the basement — bedroom closet, where?'

'Not the garage. The garage has rats and we all know Lionel boy was scared of rats —

'Donna, for Chrissake — '

'And we don't have a basement, so it can't be there — '

'Bottom line me, will you?'

' — and Lionel quit using the bedroom closet when I made him take his guns out of there — you know, on account of the kids.' She set her iron down on its pad as she was talking and now motioned for him to follow her into the bedroom. 'But you're welcome to look . . .'

Mitch searched the closet, tapping the backboard and sidewalls as well, but found nothing. He looked under the bed and behind the headboard. Again, nothing.

'This box we're looking for — what's inside it?'

'Jewelry.'

'Jewelry?'

'What're you, an echo?'

''Mean, stolen jewelry?' When Mitch nodded, Donna said: 'No way. Lionel had major problems, but ripping off jewelry wasn't one of them. You can take that to the bank.'

'Shows how well you knew him. Look,' he added before she could erupt, 'you may not like this, kiddo, but you're gonna have to get in front of it. It's not pretty,

184

but it's all part of the mess Lionel got me into up at Tahoe.' He surveyed the small room, eyes casting about for likely hiding places. 'So instead of fightin' me every inch of the way, why don't you help me look for the jewels?'

'In here? Be serious. We're so cramped, like the kids say, even the mice have moved out.'

He had to agree with her; there was barely room to squeeze between the old chipped furniture. 'Maybe you're right, maybe Lionel did hide them in his car, though I didn't see anythin' when I took his guns from the trunk.' He laughed, caustically. 'Wouldn't that be a hoot? I keep my promise to the guy and end up torching a million bucks.'

Donna gaped. 'A million? My God, who'd Lionel rob — Paris Hilton?'

'Close.'

'Well?' Donna said when Mitch didn't elaborate. 'Don't leave me hanging here. How did Lionel get his hands on a mil' worth of jewelry?'

Mitch hesitated, trying to decide if he should tell Donna everything, then said:

'They were given him as collateral.'

'Collateral on what? Come on, damn you,' she said as he hesitated again. 'I'm part of the team, remember?'

'You're better off not knowin'. Stakes this high, folks can get pretty down and dirty.'

'If you're saying my life could be in danger, my answer is — if the jewels are hidden somewhere in my house, and someone wants them back, isn't it already in danger?'

'Maybe. I don't know. What I do know is, the less you know the less danger you'll be in. And that's all I'm gonna say, so back off, okay?' He started out, then remembered something and asked: 'How're the kids takin' it?'

'Good as could be expected. A few tears and moping around, but mostly painful silence.'

'Would it be okay if I stuck my head in and said goodnight?'

Donna smiled, touched. 'It would be more than okay.'

Mitch tiptoed into an even smaller bedroom, its tiny window covered by a

186

blind and the walls by posters of rock groups and sports celebrities. That warm secret smell of children, a musky pleasant mixture of puppies and fresh-baked bread, invaded his senses. It was missing from Mitch's life and, though he had learned to live without it, he got great pleasure from being around Lionel's kids.

A nightlight glowed near his feet. It showed a boy of eight, Richie, asleep in the top bunk and his sister, Marjean, six, cuddling an armful of Beanie Bears below. Richie stirred as Mitch got close. When he saw who it was, he sat up and threw his arms about Mitch's neck. Mitch hugged him back, wishing he could be this relaxed and comfortable around women. They whispered hellos, Richie calling him Uncle Mitch, Mitch calling him Big Guy, then Marjean heard them and insisted Mitch pick her up and hug her too.

'I love you, guys — you know that, don't you?' Mitch told them. They were both in his arms and he felt them nod sleepily against his chest. 'I'm goin' to look after you.'

'You gonna look after mommy, too?'

'You betcha. Gonna look after all of you.'

'Mommy says we don't have no money.'

'Sure you do.'

'Uh-uhhh. Heard her on the phone, telling the man at the bank.'

'Well, Uncle Mitch has money, plenty of it, so quit worryin'. Like I say, we're all gonna do fine, just fine.' He hugged them again, and put them back in bed the same gentle way you put a fragile piece of china back on its shelf. Then he kissed them goodnight and started out.

Donna stood in the doorway, tears glinting in her eyes. 'Thanks,' she said as they stepped into the other room, 'they needed that.'

Mitch had no idea what to say. He hadn't known she would be listening and now that he knew he felt embarrassed.

Suddenly, in one breath, all the toughness went out of Donna. She burst into tears. 'Oh Mitch, I'm so scared. What's gonna happen to us? Other than what I make, which isn't nearly enough, we don't have a dime to fall back on.'

Mitch put his arms around her. 'Listen, what I told the kids, I meant every word. I really am gonna look after you.'

Donna nodded, head pressed to his chest.

Mitch, sensing her doubt, said: 'I got a job comin' up that'll put us on Easy Street.'

'No such place.'

'Sure there is. Just ask Dorothy and Toto.'

Donna laughed, despite her tears. 'You know, Mr. Holliday, for such a royal pain in the ass, you're really not a bad guy.'

22

The gleaming cream-and-burgundy Bentley Azure sped north along Pacific Coast Highway in the direction of Malibu. It was morning, closing in on lunch, and a misty rain blew in off the ocean. It dampened the windshield of the massive car that cost more than the gross national product of some Third World countries.

Mitch, buried in soft, buttery leather and surrounded by every luxury accessory known to man and automobile, felt uncomfortable in this climate-controlled comfort zone. He wasn't sure why — hell, being rich was part of capitalism and democracy and he was entitled to his share as much as anyone. But excessive wealth and opulence had always troubled him and now, as they purred past a GTE crew repairing telephone wires, and people in other cars pulled up alongside them at traffic lights, Mitch felt their looks said they more than just hated him for being so rich, they accused him of being responsible for all their money woes, right down to taking bread out of the mouths of their children.

Beside him, Claire experienced no such sense of guilt. Her conscience was clear as a puppy's. As she drove past the rows of expensive beachfront homes and gaudy little bungalows, separated by restaurants, nurseries and real estate offices, she was oblivious of everything, including Mitch's discomfort. Ever since she had picked him up on the corner by that ugly half-finished sailboat in the Valley, and Mitch had told her his plan about how to dispose of Edgar — starting with the phone call he'd had her make to Edgar in the Bahamas — she had scarcely been conscious of anything except making plans for the future. Finally, she was going to be free and as rich as she had always felt she should be and the mere visualization of life without any kind of restrictions made her blood race.

Her thoughts were interrupted by the gentle buzzing of the car-phone. She gave Mitch a tight-lipped glance, then, tingling all over, hit the speaker button and said: "Lo? Edgar, that you, darling?'

'Claire, I hope this is important.' He sounded irritated.

'It is. I want to throw a party when you get back.'

Although they couldn't see Edgar standing in the luxurious boardroom of the bank building in downtown Nassau, with its views of the golden beaches and glassy turquoise ocean, they could hear his voice almost strangled by fury as he said: 'You-pulled-me-away-from-a-board-meeting-to-ask-about-a-party?'

'It's not just a party, Edgar, it's an *engagement* party. *Our* engagement.' She let the words sink in before adding: 'A chance to tell all our friends how we really feel about each other.'

'I see . . . ' His anger faded.

'I've been thinking about nothing else since you left and, well, frankly, darling, I'm getting a little nervous. And I thought before I got cold feet — '

'I understand, my dear. And I think it's a great idea.'

'You do? Really?'

'Absolutely. Go ahead. Make whatever arrangements you want. You have my full blessing. Anything else?'

'Not that I can think of.'

'Well, call me if there is and I'll take care of it. Now, I've really got to get back to my meeting.'

'Of course. 'Bye, darling. Love you.' Claire shut off the speaker-phone and beamed excitedly at Mitch. 'He fell for it! The moron actually fell for it! Mitch, you're a genius.'

'Don't get carried away,' he said, wondering why he didn't share her excitement. 'Making a bear trap's easy; it's gettin' the sucker into it that makes you bite your nails.'

★   ★   ★

The rain had cleared up and the sun now shone brightly through fluffy clouds as the Bentley drove along the private road leading to the Bennett beach estate. A blue-uniformed gate-guard stepped out of his cubicle as the Bentley pulled up. Recognizing Claire, who sat alone in the

193

convertible, the guard respectfully tipped his cap. 'G'morning, Ms. Dixon. Down for some sun?'

'I wish. I'm so pale I look like a ghost.' She waited for his polite chuckle to end, and said: 'No, we're having a little shindig here in a few days. Thought I'd air the place out.'

She drove in through the gates and down a blacktop, dipping and winding across a bluff yellow with mustard grass toward a distant stand of oaks that hid all but the roof of a massive pink stucco Mediterranean villa facing the ocean.

On reaching the trees, Claire pulled over. They were now out of sight of the gate-guard. She touched a button and the trunk opened. Mitch climbed out, stretching stiffly as Claire joined him.

'You okay?' she asked, concerned. 'Not all cramped up?'

'You kiddin'? I've paid rent for dumps smaller than your trunk.'

She laughed, relieving her tension. They got back in the Bentley and drove to the villa, parking in a circular driveway that could hold fifty cars. As Mitch got out and craned his neck to get a better look of the villa, its sheer magnitude and beauty took his breath away.

'Welcome to the Pink Palace,' Claire said. 'It ain't much, but it's home.'

Mitch could only shake his head. Fitzgerald was right, he thought, the rich really are different.

The Pink Palace, according to real estate legend, was built in the thirties for a famous blonde film star who had screwed her way to the top, then boozed her career away and ended up by throwing herself off the bluff onto the rocks below. Hollywood folklore at its best. The true history of the villa was less glamorous. But it was still fascinating when one considered the original owner, a billionaire Texas oilman who had never even been to California, bought the property sight unseen, had one of his flunkies hire L.A.'s finest architect, and in a dictated letter described the home he wanted by stating: Build it bigger than Hearst Castle!

The villa was not quite that (it wasn't even the biggest house in Los Angeles county), but that did not bother the owner because he never saw it anyway; by its completion he'd lost interest in California and moved to England where he bought a one-hundred-room mansion in the country, outside London. Here, he lived in one austerely furnished wing, alone save for servants and what few family members had earned the privilege of visiting him. He died in his nineties, one of the richest men in the world but hated by everyone, not even remembering the Pink Palace by the sea that stood empty for twenty years until Edgar Bennett brought it to his wife's attention. A 'weekend beach house would be nice,' he told her and she had reluctantly driven out there with him, met the realtor, and bought the place on the spot. But Sarah, like the billionaire, never lived in it. Never even saw it a second time. She complained that it was too tiresome a drive. Besides, she hated the beach and didn't want to be anywhere but in her beloved home in San Marino. Which says something about the rich, and did nothing but enhance the local residents' opinion that Dear Old Sarah was nuttier than ten fruitcakes.

Now, as Mitch lit up a Camel and stared through his exhaled smoke at the magnificent old pink villa, Claire said: 'This is my favorite of all our homes.'

'How many do you have?'

'Five, counting the one on Long Island, which Edgar says he's selling.' She made Mitch put out his cigarette and led him up the steps. Unlocking the front door, they crossed a big flagstone entry hall and entered a spacious sunken living room. Mitch felt his shoes sink into a plush white carpet that covered about an acre of flooring until it reached the huge cathedral-style window facing the ocean. Outside, marble steps led to the bluffs. Below, a private beach sloped down to the surf. Beyond that, the ocean stretched all the way to Santa Catalina Island.

'What do you think?' Claire asked.

'I couldn't live here for a second,' Mitch said. 'It would give me claustrophobia.'

Claire laughed. 'Elaina prefers Tahoe and San Marino, and Edgar, well, he lives in the sky mostly, jetting to wherever he's got business or smells money. Which means I have this place all to myself.'

'Poor baby,' Mitch said. 'I feel sorry for you.'

Claire was not listening. Putting her arms around his neck, she kissed him. 'Just think, darling. When this mess is over, we'll be able to spend the rest of our lives here . . . with no one to bother us. Won't that be perfect?'

'Get no argument from me,' Mitch said, thinking how much he hated being called darling. 'Now, why don't you sit outside and soak up a few rays while I go do my thing and check out the alarm system.'

'All right, but don't take too long. I want you to make love to me and I don't know how long I can wait.' She kissed him again. Waited for him to slide open the glass door. Went out on the terrace.

★   ★   ★

Mitch took a notebook and pen from his pocket and went from room to room, making notes as he familiarized himself with the ground-floor alarm system. When he was finished, he went upstairs and did the same thing. Dust cloths covered the furniture in all the rooms except the master bedroom. Here, the four-poster bed, big easy chairs, armoire, and vanity table were uncovered; and when Mitch ran his finger over them, he found they were only coated with a fine layer of dust, indicating Claire or someone had been here recently. He checked out the windows and balcony French doors, all of which were protected by alarms. Nothing unusual here. But under the last window, a corner window overlooking the beach, was a glass-topped table with a chair pulled up to it. The glass was barely visible, hidden almost by a large jigsaw puzzle of a South Seas' island, with a cruise ship anchored in its harbor, all set against a magnificent sunset. The puzzle was complete save for one missing piece. Mitch dug out his wallet. Tucked inside, behind his driver's license, was the piece of red jigsaw puzzle Lionel gave him. Mitch tried it in the space in the sunset. It fitted perfectly. Mitch heard himself say: 'Hel-lo.' Removing the piece he turned it over and read for the umpteenth time: I LOVE YOU.

Well, well, well, he thought. He tucked the piece of jigsaw puzzle back in his wallet and took out his cell phone. He punched in Donna's work number, amazing himself that he knew it by heart, and when her voice came on the line, full of surprise and uneasiness because he had never called her at work, he said: 'Do me a favor, will you? Write down what I tell you and then FAX it to Sheriff Briggs up at Tahoe.'

To Donna's credit she sensed the urgency of his call, asking him no questions but just writing down what he told her and then promising to get it off right away. Mitch ended the call, went downstairs and outside to the pool area.

It had gotten warm and the glare of the sun reflecting off the water forced Mitch to put on his aviator Ray Bans. He lit up a Camel and looked about him. Two security cameras were positioned in palm trees overlooking the pool area, including the large cabana located beyond the deep end. He made note of them and entered the cabana. It was big enough to house a wet bar, 'His' and 'Her' changing rooms, showers, linen closet, and two redwood benches in front of a row of metal lockers. Piled in a corner between the door and the linen closet were several chaise lounges, their long cushions kept separate from the frames, and six inflatable rubber rafts. Everything was stacked very neatly and the thick layer of dust whitening the top cushion and the top rubber raft told Mitch they hadn't been used in months. As he took stock of the room and its contents, he heard the door open. He turned and saw Claire entering, wearing a white terrycloth robe.

'I was just comin' to get you,' he told her. Then, indicating the room: 'This is the best place to do it.'

'I agree,' she said and took off her robe.

'I meant shoot Edgar,' Mitch said, pushing her away. 'Now, rein in your hormones and let me get on with my job.'

★ ★ ★

201

Later, while they sat drinking coffee in the kitchen, Mitch saw Claire shudder and asked her what was wrong.

'I wish the party was tonight. I hate to think of Edgar touching me again . . . even for a few hours.'

The idea didn't thrill Mitch, either. 'Just hang in there, kitten. Whole thing will be over soon.'

'I wonder.'

'What's that supposed to mean?'

'Something Elaina said: that no matter how often we tried to kill Edgar, something would always crop up, go wrong and he'd go on living and torturing us forever.'

'Nothing's going to go wrong this time,' Mitch said firmly. 'Count on it.'

23

The sun was dipping behind the Santa Suzanna Mountains, reddening the calico sky above the vast floor of the Valley, when Claire dropped Mitch off on the corner by Lionel's house. In a neighborhood ruled by Detroit-born pickup trucks, vans and utility vehicles, the big gleaming Bentley, its top now down, gave the impression of royalty paying its impoverished subjects a visit, and all the kids playing in the street turned to stare.

Claire did not notice them; she was too busy looking at Mitch's unfinished sailboat. 'Can you imagine some idiot wanting to build something as ugly as that?' she said. 'And in cement too, of all things.'

Mitch shrugged. 'Maybe in the beginning,' he said, 'the guy didn't know how ugly it would turn out.'

'Could be,' she agreed. She eyed the two bearded bikers, big-bellied men in torn shirts and black leather, drinking beer on their front porch. 'But anyone who'd live across the street from a bunch of Hell's Angels, why would they care anyway?'

'Careful,' Mitch said, amused. 'I've heard they can read lips. Wouldn't want them chasing off after you.' Before Claire could react, he leaned in through the window and kissed her. 'Call me at Donna's if anything changes.'

She nodded and drove off. Mitch turned and headed for his sailboat.

In Lionel's front yard, Richie and Marjean stopped kicking a soccer ball around and ran, screaming, to Mitch. He grabbed them up, one in each arm, laughing and joking with them as he carried them to the house.

'Mom, mom,' Richie yelled as Donna opened the door for them, 'Uncle Mitch says he's gonna finish building his boat and take us all sailing.'

'Maybe even to Catalina,' Marjean put in, adding: 'Where's Catalina, momma?'

And Mitch, singing loudly off-key, 'Twenty-six miles across the sea, Santa

Catalina da-da-da-da-dee.'

And Donna laughing, saying, 'Oh God, no, spare us all, I do believe the poor man's having a seizure!' and trying to silence him by covering his mouth with both hands, the giggling kids trying to help her, Mitch trying to avoid them, and all getting entangled and tripping, losing their balance and collapsing in one gloriously happy heap on the floor.

It was a Kodak moment money could not buy.

*   *   *

It was just before dinner. Peace reigned in the house as Richie and Marjean sat watching cartoons on TV and Mitch read the *Valley Times*' sports section while Donna set the table. This weekend or next, she told Mitch, she was planning on having a garage sale. So, if he had anything he wanted to get rid of, or didn't need, set it out on the front porch. That way, she would know how much stuff there was and whether it was worth going to all the trouble of lugging everything

205

out to the sidewalk, just to make a few extra bucks. Mitch said, Okay, but he didn't think he had any worthwhile junk to get rid of. Not unless you count the Olds, Donna said. She ducked the newspaper he threw at her and ran laughing into the kitchen.

Dinner was meatloaf, mashed potatoes, gravy and peas, with low fat ice cream from 31 Flavors for dessert. Everybody cleaned their plates and afterward, while the kids grumbled over their homework, Mitch helped Donna do the dishes. By the way, she told him, Thanks for the money. What money? he asked. I didn't give you any money. Oh, she said, then it must be the gremlins again. I'll thank them next time I see them. It was a little game they played whenever Mitch had some extra cash. He always left it on top of the refrigerator, out of reach of the kids (not that they were thieves, but why tempt them, was Donna's theory), the bills held down by one of the green-frog-magnets used to stick reminders or Marjean's crayon drawings on the fridge door. Talking of money, Donna went on, if Mitch wanted to give her what he owed on his past-due telephone bill, she'd pay it for him on the way to work. Mitch thanked her and said he'd dig out the bill before going to bed. Just then, the FAX machine beeped.

'Hope that's from Briggs,' he said as he plodded into the bedroom.

He was reading the sheriff's reply to his questions, when Donna entered a few minutes later. 'What'd he say?'

Mitch's only answer was a non-committal grunt.

'Did he check on the boating accident, like you asked?'

'Uh-huh.'

'Why you interested? You think maybe the explosion wasn't an accident?' When Mitch shrugged, she said: 'Doesn't make sense. Why would Lionel kill the wife of a man he was going to work for?'

'Who said he did?'

'I don't know. I just assumed, you know, after reading your FAX — '

'Assumption's the mother of all screw-ups,' Mitch said, hoping to silence her.

'What's that, the lead-in to one of your

shade-tree parables?'

Mitch ignored her sarcasm and focused on the answers on the FAX page.

'If you didn't think Lionel was involved,' she pressed, 'why'd you ask the sheriff to check on his whereabouts the day of the accident?'

'You have a puzzle, you need to know which pieces fit where and why. Doesn't mean they all will, you understand? But you got to start somewhere, and until you got it straight which pieces do or don't belong, you can't start solving anything. Okay?'

Donna wasn't satisfied. Thinking back, she said, 'I never understood why he took that job in the first place. He hated being a chauffeur. And he hated driving for Edgar Bennett even more.'

'Elaina, you mean?'

'Her, too. Said they both treated him like dirt.'

'You sure about that?' Mitch said, confused. 'That Lionel drove for Bennett as well as Elaina?'

'Absolutely.'

'Before or after the accident?'

'Before. About six months, I think. I kept telling him to quit, but he wouldn't. Said he was onto a good thing.'

'Meaning?'

'Beats me. The money wasn't that great and the hours sucked. Sometimes he was gone all night and would come home looking like something the cat dragged in. But that didn't stop Lionel, dumb jerk. Kept acting like he was going to be a millionaire some day — ' She broke off as something dawned on her, then exclaimed: 'Oh-my-God.'

'What?'

'You think maybe Edgar Bennett promised Lionel a million bucks if he'd kill his wife? Nah,' she said, before Mitch could answer, 'that wouldn't make sense. Bennett hadn't gotten his paws on the Dixon millions then — '

'Sure he had. Mrs. Dixon married Edgar long before the boat blew up.'

'Yeah, but according to Lionel, there was a major court battle going on — you know, who was going to control the family fortune — Bennett or the daughters.' She smiled, amused by her thoughts. 'Seems

Momma Dearest was as whacky as Elaina and the girls' lawyers were trying to prove she wasn't competent enough to know who was capable of deciding who should manage the estate. What?' Donna added, seeing Mitch' expression. 'Why the look?'

'Nothin'.'

'Nothing, my ass. You look like I just gave you the winning ticket for the lottery.'

You did, Mitch thought. Aloud, he said: 'Donna, stop playing detective.'

'Then, tell me what the hell's going on.'

'I will — soon as I figure it out myself.' He tucked the FAX into his pocket, went back into the living room and sat down to watch a *Seinfeld* rerun on TV, thinking: *I shouldn't spend so much time over here. Donna and I, we're getting too close. Next thing you know, she'll expect a goddamn wedding ring and then I'll be trapped just like Lionel was and not only that, I won't be able to live on the boat anymore because it'll be too awkward. And if I don't live close I won't be able to see the kids again and I do so love those kids. Jesus.*

They were watching the ten o'clock news on Channel 9 when the call came. Donna answered on the first ring, hoping not to wake up the kids. After listening for only a few moments, she held the receiver out to Mitch, her expression saying it was bad news before he even knew who the caller was.

'Yeah, who's this?'

It was Claire, her voice so shrill and stressed-out he barely recognized it. She tried to tell him what had happened but was too panicked to make any sense, and Mitch had to keep making her repeat herself before he finally got the whole picture. Bottom line, Elaina had wigged out on booze and pills, taken the limo and crashed it through the gates and driven off, vanishing into the night before Mace or Taggert could stop her; and now, after they had spent two hours searching for her and had come up empty, the police had called and said they'd found the big Mercedes stretch abandoned in the parking lot of the U.S. Court of Appeals building.

'Do you know where that is, Mitch?' Claire asked.

'Sure. It's that big pinkish-red building overlooking the Arroyo Seco. Used to be the old Vista del Arroyo Hotel. Was there any sign of Elaina?'

'No. And I didn't tell them what she'd done, or say she was missing or anything, so they — the police, I mean — don't know she was involved, think someone just stole the limo and towed it to their compound, wherever the hell that is, so I sent Taggert and Mace over there to pick it up and, Oh God, dear God, I don't know what to do or know if I even did the right thing, not telling them, I don't know, it all happened so fast and just at the wrong time, it's as if Fate's doing it again, saving Edgar, I mean, like Elaina said would happen and — '

'Hold it,' Mitch said. 'Stop right there. Let's not worry about Fate right now, let's just concentrate on Elaina.'

'Yes, yes, you're exactly right, that's what I want us to do, find Elaina before she does something awful and the police pick her up and arrest her, then the shit will hit the fan and we won't be able to cover it up, be too late and all over the news and when Edgar gets back and hears about it, he'll go ballistic and want to have her committed and there goes the party and any chance we'll have of doing it, you know, getting rid of him and — '

'Enough,' Mitch told her. 'Just shut up and listen.'

'But — '

'LISTEN, GODDAMMIT!'

Then as she fell silent:

'I'll handle this.'

'How?'

Hating what he was about to say but knowing it was the safest way out, Mitch said: 'I'll drive over there now, try to round Elaina up. Way she looks, and the shape you say she's in, shouldn't be too hard to find her. I mean she can't get too far on crutches.'

'Maybe I should go with you?'

'No.'

'You don't understand. Elaina, she can be an awful handful when she's like this and I'm the only one she'll let do anything with her.'

About to say 'no' again, Mitch remembered the police and how he didn't want any problems or notoriety right now. 'Okay, tell you what,' he said. 'If I find her and can't get her home, I'll call you, tell you where I'm at, and you can come and get her, okay?'

'If you think that's best — '

'I do. Now, hang up so I can get the hell out here. Sooner I find her, sooner this nightmare's over.'

'Yes, yes, but . . . '

'But, what?'

'There's something else, Mitch — something I didn't tell you.'

He wanted to strangle her. 'So tell me now.'

'Elaina left a note on her bed.'

'What'd it say?'

'Goodbye . . . '

'Christ!' He banged down the phone.

Donna looked at him, concerned, but knowing enough not to say a word.

Mitch read her expression and said with a shrug of his heavy shoulders: 'Hey, it's what I do. Clean up other people's shit.'

He was gone before she could even wish him luck.

24

Freeways, when rush hour does not turn them into horn-honking parking lots, are a great way to get somewhere in a hurry. Now, with the dash-clock of his '82 Thunderbird reading 11:17, Mitch got onto the 134 east and cut across the Valley in the direction of Pasadena. There was very little traffic and he did eighty most of the way. It gave him time to think. The U.S. Court of Appeals Building was closed at this hour, so what was Elaina doing there? Meeting someone to run away with, he wondered. If so, who? If not, why abandon the limo there and walk to wherever she was going? No matter how close her destination was, it would be a chore on crutches. And why write a note saying 'goodbye' when all that would do is bring Bennett's watchdogs, Mace and Taggert, chasing after her? It didn't make sense.

Ahead, alongside the freeway on his

right, the Colorado Street Bridge loomed up. Built in 1913, the big concrete structure spanned a large ravine called the Arroyo Seco and was notable for its distinctive Beaux Arts arches, antique lampposts and railings. It was also notable, Mitch remembered as he looked at it, for the more than one hundred people who had taken a header off it, giving it the nickname: 'Suicide Bridge.'

Then it hit him. *Holy Christ*, he thought. *Elaina wasn't running away — she intended to kill herself.*

Slamming on the brakes, he veered across traffic and dived down the San Rafael exit ramp. Turning right, he drove to Colorado Boulevard and followed it to the bridge. There was a moon and by its light he could see the dome-topped tower of the massive, Spanish-colonial U.S. Court of Appeals building perched on the crest of the hill across the ravine.

He could also see the entrance to the bridge. Braking, he drove across the first span and almost immediately saw a slender white-gowned figure clinging to one of the antique lampposts poking above the metal 'suicide fence.' It was Elaina: he knew that before he even caught sight of her face.

If she saw him, or the car, she showed no sign of it. She continued to cling to the lamppost, bare feet resting on the concrete base, staring out over the dark, wooded ravine one hundred and fifty feet below.

Stopping beside her, Mitch climbed out of his car and walked up to her. Again, she showed no sign of noticing him. Moving slowly, so as not to alarm her, he entered the little square-shaped alcove beside the lamppost and smiled at her.

'Well, well,' he said gently, 'if it isn't Miss Tinkerbelle.'

'Go 'way,' she said without looking at him. 'I don' wan' you here, Holden.' Her words were slurred and, if he could have seen her eyes, he would have realized alcohol and drugs had turned them glazed and dreamy.

''Mean you'd deprive me of watchin' you fly?'

'I can, y'know,' she said. 'Wanna see me?'

'Sure.' He peered through the metal fence at the dark ravine below. 'First, though, let's pick out where you're gonna land. I know — what about that big bush there? See,' he pointed, 'on the left. Think you can make a three-point landing?'

She didn't answer for a moment. Then turning her head just enough to see him, she said: 'Stop makin' fun of me, Holden.'

'Now why would I do that, princess? Hell, I got out of bed to come here an' see you fly.' As he spoke he inched closer to her. Now less than two feet separated them and he got ready to grab her.

'Stop!' she suddenly screamed. 'Don'-come-any-closer!'

Ignoring her, he lunged for her legs.

At that moment Elaina let go of the lamppost, spread her arms like wings and jumped.

Mitch felt his outstretched hands bump against her gowned thighs and thought he'd lost her. But as his hands slid down her bare calves, he made a second desperate grab for her. His fingers closed around her ankles and he yanked backward, using his weight to stop her from falling.

Elaine's scream echoed throughout the dark ravine. Mitch felt himself jerked forward, his chest slamming against the railing, one of the suicide-fence spikes grazing his cheek.

But he still had hold of her ankles and he pulled her back to safety. Both went sprawling to the ground. She fought him, kicking and punching him with her gloved fists.

Mitch yelled at her to cut it out, but she only struggled harder; and finally he had no choice but to clip her on the jaw. She went limp in his arms. He pushed her aside and sat there a moment, chest heaving, wondering how the hell he got himself into these kind of messes. Because you're an idiot, he told himself. An idiot who never learns from his mistakes! Rising, he wearily picked up Elaina's crutches and threw them in the car.

Elaina hadn't moved. But as Mitch buckled her into the passenger seat, she came around long enough to mumble a few unintelligible words. About to clip her on the jaw again, he lowered his cocked fist as she passed out and slumped against the door.

Lighting a cigarette, Mitch got into the car, drove across the bridge to the freeway on-ramp and headed for Pasadena.

It had been some night.

25

When Mitch pulled up to the entrance to the Bennett estate in San Marino, the T-bird headlights showed the damaged electric gates had been dragged together and chained in the middle. The Mercedes limo was parked in the driveway. Before Mitch could honk, Taggert got out, came to the gates, unhooked the chain and opened one side so Mitch could drive through.

Mitch had called Claire from the car during the ride home. He saw her now, waiting for him on the front steps of the mansion. With her stood a tall, elegant, silver-haired man of fifty wearing eight-hundred-dollar Cartier gold-framed glasses and a gray cashmere sports coat thrown over FILA sweats. He looked irritated, as if he were there only because he had to be, and Mitch guessed even before he got out and Claire introduced them, that he was the family doctor.

'How long's she been this way, unconscious?' he asked Mitch as Mace carried Elaina into the mansion.

''Bout ten minutes.'

The little group headed upstairs.

'Any idea what she ingested before she passed out?'

'No to the first question,' Mitch said; 'and she didn't pass out, I gave her a little tap on the chin.' He was ready to defend his actions if anyone challenged him but Elaina's bizarre behavior was so well documented, by now everyone was immune to it and accepted anything that happened to her as if it were part of the norm.

Once they got her in bed, Mitch, Claire, and Mace left her in the expert-but-uncaring hands of Dr. Seymore Braithwaite. Claire told Mace to stand guard outside the door for the rest of the night. Then she led Mitch downstairs into the library. The huge dignified room had stained-glass French doors that opened out onto the terraced pool, smelled of brandy and cigars, and was lined with famous literary works that looked as if they had been bought by the ton. Claire fixed herself and Mitch a double Scotch without asking if he wanted anything and they drank it in silence, not even looking at each other, seated on a massive couch facing the fireplace. As they got comfortable, the leather creaked and sighed, as if greeting old friends, and for the first time since Claire had called him, Mitch felt himself relax.

'God, what a night,' Claire said finally. 'I can't thank you enough. You know that, don't you?' When he didn't answer, she closed her eyes and leaned her head back, hair spilling softly over Mitch's shoulder, and didn't speak for so long he thought she'd gone to sleep. He was in no hurry to say anything himself. He was content to just sit there sipping the expensive Glenmorangie Scotch and letting his mind wander over the events of the night.

Finally, he said: 'When'd she start wearing gloves?'

Claire, without opening her eyes, said: 'What?'

'Those white cotton gloves — when did

Elaina start wearing them?'

'I don't know. Few days ago.'

'Think she's trying to hide the marks on her palms?'

Claire opened her eyes. 'You saw them?'

Mitch nodded. 'I took a look as we were driving here.'

'What d'you think?'

'Could be anything, like you said.'

'Anything but nails, wouldn't you say?'

'Nails?'

'Roman nails. Get it?'

'Christ,' Mitch said.

'Exactly.' Claire closed her eyes, lay back against Mitch's shoulder and said: 'I'm sorry I dragged you into this.'

'It's okay.'

'I had no one else to turn to and I knew if we didn't find her, get her back here before the police did, we wouldn't be able to sweep all the crap under the carpet without Edgar finding out.'

'I said it's okay.' Closing his eyes, he smelled wet lilacs and heard leather creaking as she moved close and pressed her lips against his cheek.

'I'll make it up to you, Mr. Mitchell Holliday — I promise. We'll have a life together the angels will envy.'

Then, when he did not say anything:

'You do still want me, don't you?'

'What d'you think?'

'I think if I lost you now, I'd die.'

I feel the same way, he thought, *maybe more so and that's dangerous because I may have trouble if I ever want to rein myself in.*

The door opened and the elegant Dr. Braithwaite entered, his tanned bare feet tucked into Bruno Magli loafers. He gave Claire a smile that Mitch found ingratiating and said he'd examined Elaina and except for a few scratches there was nothing wrong with her. Just to be sure she was all right, though, he'd send one of his nurses to check on her tomorrow.

'No, Seymour,' Claire said firmly. 'I want *you* to come.'

'Claire, I can't — '

'*You,* not some hired nurse. Understand? *You.*'

They locked gazes. The battle of wits lasted less than a heartbeat.

'Very well, my dear.' Dr. Braithwaite smiled, showing two rows of perfectly capped teeth. It was his bedside smile, a smile that was charming below his nose but never reached his cold gray eyes. 'See you tomorrow, then. Goodnight, all.'

'Smarmy bastard,' Claire said when he was gone. 'The retainer we pay him, the least the prick could do was *pretend* like he cared.'

Mitch finished his drink and suddenly had to get out of there.

'Where're you going?'

'Home.'

'Do you have to?'

'Yes,' he said, saying it in a way that made her understand that nothing she could say would change his mind. 'Call you tomorrow.'

26

During the drive back to Reseda, Mitch, mind racing a lot faster than the T-bird was traveling, made a decision; and having made it, forgot about it and thought only about collapsing into bed and sleeping around the clock. He pretended it was because he was exhausted, but he had never been good at lying to himself and he knew it was really because he was worried about what he might do in the days ahead. Screw it, he thought then. You'll do what you always do. Make a decision and live with it. Trust yourself.

He felt better then and for the rest of the drive he listened to the beautiful soft sad sounds of Wynton Marsalis playing jazz on his trumpet as only he could, God bless him.

★　★　★

Donna sat on her bed in the dark, peering out through the blind. She'd been waiting for Mitch to return for over an hour. At first, she had not been too worried. Mitch was no choirboy, he was tough and he'd been around. But as time passed and Mitch didn't show, she started to picture all the bad things that could happen to him; worse, despite being a normally positive person, the more she tried to dismiss them, the worse they became until now she knew, just *knew* Mitch was dead.

But Fate was in a playful mood tonight and toyed with Donna's emotions. She had barely convinced herself that Mitch was gone when headlights flooded over the chain-link gate. Her heart leapt, then sank. She held her breath. Was it the police coming to tell her the bad news or . . . ?

But it was Mitch, all right, using the bumper of his T-bird to gently nudge the gate open and then driving on through and parking between the tarp-covered Olds and his unfinished sailboat.

Relief flooded through her. She wanted

to run to him, to throw her arms around his neck and kiss him and tell him how much she loved him; but she didn't because she sensed this gruff bear of a man, a guy who was so gentle and tender inside (so in need of someone to love him, she hoped) that he hid his emotions under a veneer of toughness for fear of being hurt — would mistake her intentions and think she was crowding him and then she'd lose him forever; so she merely thanked God for answering her prayers, got up, calmly took off her robe, spread it over the blanket for extra warmth against the night's chill, and got into bed.

She was asleep almost before her head hit the pillow.

27

Friday dawned clear and blustery. A Santa Ana had sprung up during the night. The powerful gusts of wind brought a crackling dryness to the Los Angeles basin that would have people grumbling throughout the day about getting zapped by static electricity every time they touched something. But the good news was that the smog was gone. It was one of those golden-blue days that make the rest of the country envious; a day when everything sparkled and gleamed like the ocean after the rain, and drivers coming over the San Diego hill into the Valley could see as far as their eyes let them, picking out leaves on distant trees, windows in buildings they never knew existed before and, way across the sprawled-out Valley floor, the purple-and-brown mountains looking so clear you felt you could reach out and touch them.

But for most Valley-dwellers, the high

wind was nothing but a big fat pain in the butt. It meant frequent power shortages, roads blocked by uprooted trees, just-raked lawns buried under leaves and, worst of all, for those who had allergies, it meant clogged sinuses and a day spent sneezing and rubbing red, puffy eyes that never stopped watering.

Mitch knew the Santa Anas were blowing the instant he awoke and realized he couldn't breathe through his nose. He also had a headache that made something as simple as lifting his head off the pillow excruciating.

But there was worse news: presently Donna banged on the side of the sailboat and, when Mitch looked out of the cabin to see what she wanted, he saw even before she told him that a branch had broken off one of the walnut trees and landed onto the hood of his beloved Olds. He wanted to let loose a mouthful of profanity. But the kids were with Donna, who was dropping them off at school on her way to work; so he just stood there, silently apoplectic, hearing nothing she said or even the kids saying 'Bye, Uncle

Mitch,' but knowing, just knowing, that this was going to be one of those days!

*   *   *

The moron at the body-shop where Mitch later took the Olds to get an estimate didn't help put out any fires, either. He spoke about the dented white hood as if it were nothing, as if he were talking about some old beat-up truck, not a restored classic, even going so far as to cheerfully say that Mitch was one lucky sumbitch the wind didn't blow the tarp off the car or the damage would've been much worse. No, Mitch said, wanting to kill him. He wasn't lucky. He wasn't lucky at all. Lucky sumbitches didn't have goddamn trees fall on their goddamn cars in the goddamn first place.

*   *   *

That morning there was a six-car pile up on the Pasadena freeway. Mitch, trapped in the traffic waiting for the CHP and tow-trucks to clear away the wreck, told himself that maybe he was lucky after all — if he hadn't been delayed he might have been part of the accident instead of an observer. But this attempt to justify his undeserved misfortune didn't really do it for Mitch and he arrived at the Bennett mansion in San Marino still steamed and in no shape to plan a murder.

The maid who answered the door said Miss Claire was waiting for him and led Mitch out on the terrace. Claire, he realized, was one of those rare people who could look stressed out while reclined in a lounge chair. She'd been expecting him all morning, she said as he sat beside her. What the hell happened? Don't ask, he told her. You don't want to know. Yes, I do, she said. I want to know everything about you. She pressed her hand fondly over his as she spoke, took off her sunglasses and looked at him from under long, lowered lashes. Her eyes said she loved him and Mitch, feeling her heat, found himself explaining about the branch falling on the Olds.

'Poor sweetie,' she said. 'What an awful

thing to happen.' She went on to explain that she knew exactly how he felt, having recently lost her cat, Snowball, to coyotes. She'd cried for days and even signed a petition circulating the neighborhood demanding the Animal Regulation Department get off their butts and exterminate the coyotes that seemed to think cats were part of the natural food chain. Mitch couldn't see the connection, but then he wasn't a cat lover. He also thought it was strange, damned strange, the two of them sitting there in the warm morning sun talking about Oldsmobiles and cats when really all they had on their minds was whacking Edgar.

Not wanting to be the first one to mention it, he changed the subject and asked how Elaina was. Still asleep, Claire said. She added that Braithwaite had probably shot her sister full of sedatives so he wouldn't have to bother with her for the rest of the day.

Mitch was surprised. Braithwaite had already been here? Sure, Claire said. Arrived at the crack of dawn. Claimed he was on his way to the hospital. But she knew better, remembering that on Fridays the good doctor played an early round of golf at the country club. Only reason he'd stopped by early was to annoy her, knowing she liked to sleep late. Also, because he'd 'taken time out of his busy schedule,' she now couldn't bad-mouth him to Edgar as an uncaring, money-grabbing suck-up who didn't care about anybody but himself and should have his license revoked. She sounded so incensed, Mitch wondered if there wasn't another, more personal reason she hated Braithwaite. But when he asked her, she said no, that if either one of them had reason to hate the other, it was Braithwaite because he'd once asked her to marry him and she turned him down. Then, as if the subject upset her, she excused herself and went indoors.

When she returned, she had changed from her jeans and sweater to an elegant cream pantsuit and seemed to have forgotten all about Braithwaite. She asked Mitch if he minded being alone for a little while; her secretary had arrived and they needed to go over the arrangements for

the party tomorrow night. She empha-
sized the word 'party' and gave Mitch a
look that pronounced Edgar's doom.

'Go ahead,' he told her. 'I'll lie here an'
get some sun.'

'If you get hungry, darling, go in and
ask the cook to fix you something,
anything you want.' She kissed him,
whispered 'one more day,' and was gone.

Mitch lay back, closed his eyes, felt the
sun warming his face and dozed off
thinking how easy it would be to slide
right into this way of life. No more money
problems, just enjoying every day as it
came, pampered by maids, cooks and
chauffeurs and knowing everywhere you
went you'd go first class and be catered to
and welcomed, no matter what you said
or did, because no one could afford to
cross you. Not a bad way to go . . .

And all he had to do to get it was shoot
Edgar tomorrow. He would be doing the
world a service, too; ridding it of an
unconscionable pervert who had killed
his wife, crippled one stepdaughter and
was trying to force the other to marry
him. If there was ever justification for

murder, Fate had handed it to Mitch, along with a chance for luxury beyond his wildest dreams and the love of a beautiful woman —

Mitch's daydreaming was interrupted by the maid tugging on his arm and saying Miss Elaina wanted to see him. Rising, he followed Teresa into the mansion.

28

Upstairs, Taggert was on guard outside Elaina's door. He showed no hostility toward Mitch, but nodded as if they were old friends and opened the door for him. 'She wants to thank you, Ace,' Taggert said.

'Lucky me,' Mitch said as he entered the large sunny room. For a moment he thought he had stepped into FAO Schwartz. Bears, lions, giraffes, frogs, dinosaurs, you name it, they were there, all lovingly arranged about the room, ranging in size from a tiny blue mouse to a green gorilla bigger than Mitch. In the center of the room, like a magical pink-and-white island floating on a plum-colored carpet, was a giant round bed. On it, Elaina lay propped up by pillows cuddling an old faded brown teddy bear with silver-button eyes that didn't match. Years of loving had abused the stuffing inside the bear, giving it a sad, misshapen body, flopped-over ears and a sorry pushed-in smile.

But, bad as the bear looked, Elaina looked worse. She wore no makeup, her red hair wasn't brushed, and her green eyes had sunken so far into their sockets they seemed to be imprisoned by the dark circles surrounding them. Clutched in one white-gloved hand was a King James edition of the Holy Bible.

'How you feeling, princess?'

'On top of the world.'

'That bad, huh?'

'Now we're getting somewhere,' she said. 'Never shit a shitter, eh, Holden?' She sucked on her thumb, which protruded through a hole she'd chewed in the glove, and giggled. 'Are you happy you saved me?'

'Delirious.'

She gave an ugly little laugh that twisted the corners of her pale, full-lipped mouth. 'Crazy thing is I don't remember anything. Can you believe that, not one thing. Not busting out of here, not crashing the limo through the gates, not whatever I did outside, not you bringing me home, nothing, you understand. Zilch, zippo, nada. Nothing. How about that?'

'How 'bout that.'

She shot him a look that should have shriveled him. 'I hate you, you know that?'

'The line's getting longer every day.'

'I carefully planned last night, wanted it to be my last hurrah, so to speak. You know, like Jesus on the cross.'

'I thought you were Tinkerbelle learnin' to fly?'

She went on as if he had not spoken. 'No nails through my hands but landing *ker-splat* on the ground with my arms and legs spread-eagled like I was pinned to a crucifix.'

'Is that why you're wearing those gloves — to hide the holes?'

'You know about the holes?' Elaina looked surprised.

'Just answer the question.'

'Yes.' She held both hands up, palms toward him. 'When I woke up this morning, the holes were there and the gloves were all bloody.'

'Not bloody now.'

'I know. And the holes are gone, too.'

'How do you explain that?'

'I can't.' She saw his look and said nastily: 'I was wrong about you, Holden. You're just another ignorant doubter, like the rest of the flock.'

'Why? 'Cause I think you're imagining things?'

''Cause you can't see past your nose. Don't you get it, Holden, I'm here for a special reason, God's reason, even if I'm the only one who knows it.'

She paused and Mitch wondered how he could get out of there without pushing her over the edge, if she was not over already.

'That reason was set up for me last night,' she continued, 'but you, you near-sighted Philistine, you spoiled all that. You took away my one shining moment and now I doubt if I'll ever get another chance, not the way it's looking, which, from where I sit, is through the bars of some rich man's loony bin; unless, of course, I can drag my butt out of this bed and convince darling Claire to let me go to the party — which of course she won't do, the bitch. She's too afraid I'll say or do something that'll fuck things up between her and Popsie. Not that I care, really, he deserves what he gets, they both deserve what they get in fact, though no one but me will ever say it.'

She closed her eyes and seemed to wind down.

'I ought to go, so you can get some rest.'

She wasn't having it. 'Ever a day go by you didn't want to kill yourself?' she said as if he hadn't spoken.

'A few.'

'You're lucky. I've been trying one way or another since I was born. No, check that, since the accident, and I realized God had decided to make me a martyr — you know, one of the favored, the chosen. That's what we are, you know: His chosen. Bring me your tired, your huddled masses — '

'I think that's the Statue of Liberty.'

'Same thing, different woman. God *is* a woman, you know.'

'That's what I told Lionel.'

'You did?' She giggled. 'What did he say?'

'Pretty much took it in stride.'

'Good for him. See,' she added, 'the way it goes, if God makes you a cripple, you got it made. A front row seat in heaven. E-ride all the way, Holden.'

'E-ride? How do you know about E-rides at your age? They went out of fashion more than twenty years ago.'

'Jesus told me about them.

'Why didn't I think of that?'

'Same time that Jesus told me dear ol' Walt had bought up all the E-rides years ago when those jerks raised the prices at Disneyland. First thing he did when he passed through the gates was to sell them to God at a discount,' she suddenly broke off as if hearing herself, then asked: 'Am I making any sense, here?'

'Does it matter?' Mitch said.

''Course it matters, you jerk-off. I start making sense and my whole world goes into the toilet.'

'Why's that?'

''Cause I'm crazy and crazies aren't supposed to make sense. Crazies are only out there for one thing, the enjoyment of others. Any time you forget that, start thinking differently, God up and whacks you alongside the head just to remind you, to straighten out your brains.'

'You really should get some rest,' Mitch said.

'Fuck you and your hundred'n-twenty white horses, courtesy of Dodge.' She saw his eyebrows arch, and giggled. 'Didn't think I remembered, did you? Well, I did, do. First thing you ever said to me. On the stairs, remember?'

'How could I forget?'

'No, no, don't wimp out on me now, Holden. Only no-brain pricks are condescending. Be yourself. Be honest. You're one of a kind. An original, don't you see? So, tell me the truth. You're surprised I remembered, aren't you?'

'No,' Mitch said, 'not really.'

'You aren't? Why not?'

'Ever hear the story 'bout the man who had a flat outside the insane asylum? A kid runs up and steals all the lug nuts while he's changing the tire. Well, he's sitting there wondering what to do when an inmate leans out the window and says, Why don't you take one nut from all the other wheels, put them all on that one, then you'll have four on each wheel and can drive to a gas station. Well, the guy's so impressed he says, If you can figure something like that out, how come you're in there? And the looney says, Hey, man, I'm may be crazy, but I ain't stupid.'

'A parable. How fitting. From your lips to God's ears.' Elaina giggled and sucked her thumb. 'That's cute,' she said. 'You're cute. But you already know that, don't you?'

'Just like you know you're not stupid.'

'Yes,' she said, in a voice that echoed of sanity, 'I know that, all right. What worries me, though, could I really be crazy like my mom?'

'Not in my book.'

'Then why do I do what I do?'

'You'll have to ask someone a lot smarter than me to find that out.'

'Don't underestimate yourself. You're a lot smarter than any shrink I ever went to. 'Least you can get me to talk about myself.'

'Maybe. But I don't have the brains to cure you.'

'Who says I want to be cured? Maybe I like being the only dodo out there on a limb.'

'Do you?'

'What do you think?'

'Only you can answer that. But it can get pretty lonely at times. I know, I been there.'

'And that makes you an expert?'

She was getting mean and he knew it was time to leave.

'See you around, princess. Take care.'

'Damn you,' she said. 'Now you've made me sad again, Holden.' Tears suddenly ran down her face. Mitch melted. He sat beside her, held her tight like the little girl she was and did his best to soothe her. He did okay. Elaine fell asleep in his arms; and after awhile he was able to gently lower her onto the pillow and walk out, leaving her sleeping soundly.

★   ★   ★

It was long after midnight when she called. Mitch, tucked in his bunk in the unfinished sailboat, was sleeping far sounder than a man with his problems deserved. He and Claire had spent the afternoon discussing his plan to kill Edgar. He had then driven back to the Valley, stopping in at the body-shop to check on the Olds. Then picking up some Koo-Koo-Roo chicken, he had taken it back to the boat. A note pinned on the stepladder told him Donna and the kids had gone to see a movie. A P.S. added that she'd paid his telephone bill so his phone should be working. He tried it and got a line. He blessed Donna, ate his dinner, and watched TV until he fell asleep. Donna driving in with the kids woke him up shortly after nine. He contemplated going over the house to talk to her, decided he was too tired to answer any of her questions, and went back to sleep.

Now, wakened out of a dead sleep by Elaina's call, he fumbled around until he found the phone under the bunk, said: ''Lo?''

'It's me, your friendly Jesus Freak. You asleep?'

'Not anymore. What's wrong?'

'Nothing. For the first time in a long time, there's absolutely nothing wrong.'

'Thanks for calling to tell me that.'

'That's what dodos do. Call you when it's all going so good, it's scary.'

'Sorry, I forgot. Been a while since I knew any dodos.'

'You're cute, you know that?' She giggled and though he couldn't see her, he knew she was sucking her thumb.

'But that's not why you called.'

'Silly, 'course not. I wanted to ask you a question.'

'Fire away.'

'Ever read Dostoyevsky's *The Idiot*?

'Sure. Every morning before my Wheaties.'

'It's about this simple-minded Russian peasant with the virtues of a saint.'

'And you're suggesting I read this because — ?'

She ignored him; said: 'How about *Catcher In The Rye*?'

'Nope.'

'You should read it. It's all about you.'

'I thought it was about a kid in college.'

'That's just on the surface. It's what's between the lines that really matters. Same as in *The Idiot*. The world sees him as a feeble-minded klutz one step from a funny farm but in reality, like Holden in *Catcher*, he's pure saint.'

'So I'm St. Simple Simon, the village idiot — that what you're saying?'

'Damn you. Now you're not being cute at all.'

'Sorry. Just trying to get a handle on things.'

'Then read the goddamn books, you'll see what I mean.' She banged down the receiver.

Mitch sighed, hung up, and fell asleep wondering how she got his number.

29

Saturday morning, the Santa Ana was still blowing but with less force. But strong enough to stir up the pollen, giving people with allergies fits. Mitch took his sinus medication and tried to go back to sleep. His headache was pounding too hard for that, but what the hell, he thought as he lay there dozing, what's a goddamn headache compared to what he was going to do tonight?

He reached for the phone then remembered that Claire had told him not to call her today in case Edgar overheard her talking and became suspicious. What about Armani and Boss, Mitch had asked her. What about them, she said. You don't think they'll spill the beans, tell Bennett I was here and was the one who brought Elaina home? What, and blow a million a piece? I don't think so. Mitch was stunned. Christ, is that what you're paying them to keep quiet? Man, that's a pretty pricey gag order. It's worth it, she said. Lose two to keep five hundred. I'll take those odds any day. Mitch would have, too, except in his world he couldn't even fathom that much money; like asking someone other than an astronomer how far six trillion light years was — it existed, you supposed, because they, the ones with the brains, said it did; but as far as really grasping what it meant, no way. Try as you might, you couldn't. It was too mind-boggling.

In his mind Claire was now saying in a thin flat voice that made Mitch shiver, 'Anyway, maybe I will, maybe I won't — pay them, I mean. I'll cross that bridge when I come to it.'

So, Mitch thought, one murder isn't her limit? Before even one man was dead she was already considering taking out two more. Just like that, a snap of the fingers. And for a lousy two million that, like she'd said, wasn't more than a piss in the bucket when you had five hundred mil left to play with. Sweet Jesus, life truly was different when you were mega-rich. You could buy your way out of anything.

The phone rang, canceling his thoughts. It was Donna, asking him if he would like to come over for pancakes. Is the Pope Catholic, he replied. My God, she said. Don't you ever hire new writers? Talk about stale clichés . . .

It was the start of a bad morning for them. He tried to deflect any more trouble by giving the kids each a toy, a Barbie doll for Marjean and a miniature replica of a Jeff Gordon stock car for Richie. He had picked the gifts up at a mini-mall a few days prior to going to Lake Tahoe with Lionel, but because of everything that had happened recently he had forgotten all about them. The kids were overjoyed and hugged him like he'd given them a free pass to Disneyland.

Donna, too, was touched by his thoughtfulness. He could tell that by the way she squeezed his hand for a moment and mouthed 'thank you' to him; but that did not mean she wasn't still upset with him. She sensed more than knew he was about to do something dangerously stupid and it made her crazy that he refused to talk about it.

'Lionel always used to tell me what he was up to,' she said, lying and knowing that Mitch knew she was lying.

'Lionel's dead,' Mitch said. 'Is that what you want, Donna, me dead with him?'

'Then you admit that what you're doing is dangerous?'

'I admit nothing.'

'Why won't you tell us, Uncle Mitch?' Richie asked.

''Cause then it wouldn't be a secret, Big Guy. A secret's only a secret if one person knows about it.'

'Momma says we're not s'posed to keep secrets,' Marjean said, chiming in.

'So you shouldn't, sweetheart. But Donna isn't my mom, so it's different for me. Now,' he said to Donna, 'okay we change the subject so I can enjoy my pancakes?'

She did not answer. Nor did she bring up the subject again during breakfast. But Mitch knew it wasn't over. And, sure enough, he had not been back on the boat for more than ten minutes when over she came, climbing aboard and descending into the little cramped cabin without her customary cheerful 'Coming aboard, skipper', so that he knew she was still riled even before she opened her mouth.

'Don't go there,' he warned as she sat across the tiny fold-up table from him. 'This is none of your damn' business, so just shut up about it or get ashore.'

Tears glinted in her sad dark eyes.

'That won't work, either,' he said, though it was working already and he was just stalling, trying to stop her before he made a fool of himself and melted in front of her.

'Will you at least tell me this, then?' she begged.

'I don't know. Depends what it is.'

'Are you doing what you're doing because of us, the kids and me, I mean, 'cause of what I said about our not having any future?'

'No,' he lied. 'Absolutely not. What I'm doing has nothing to do with you or the kids, it's strictly for *moi*.'

'How about the blonde in the Bentley — she involved?'

'Leave her out of it.'

'How can I?' Donna said. 'She's about to steal the man I love and there's not one thing I can do about it.' She stood up, tears running down her cheeks, climbed off the boat and headed back to the house.

Damn, he thought. *Why did everything he touched seem to turn to shit?*

30

The one thing Mitch had going for him, the thing that had saved his butt on more than one occasion and made him dangerous, was: he knew he wasn't too swift when it came to figuring things out. He never had been. Not as a kid, not in school, not in the workplace, not even when he decided to become a private dick. Never!

At first, when his dad had told him, 'You ain't no whiz kid, pal, not in the brain department, never will be neither, so don't try'n kid yourself you are 'cause you'll only get hurt, maybe killed, just be happy you can take a punch and get up swingin' and you'll do okay,' Mitch had gone into denial. But gradually, over the years, he'd learned his lesson, painfully, finally accepting himself for what he was and nothing more, and then wisely doing what smarter people would've done at once, turned a disadvantage into an advantage; become patient with himself and let his problems stew awhile instead of rushing in to solve them.

It was not pretty, but it worked. Mitch had survived everything Fate and his own poor judgment had thrown at him.

He had shot people — muggers, junkies, bail-skippers, and their kind — killed a cop, and once, during a fight in a bar, he'd belted a drunk coming at him with a broken bottle and the kid had gone down hard, hitting his head on the wall and bought the music even though Mitch had called the paramedics and they'd done their damnedest to keep him alive. Turned out the drunk was a decorated war veteran. His death had kept Mitch awake at night for a long time.

And now, Mitch thought as he walked along Malibu beach in the dark, he was about to commit murder.

The Big M.

For a shot at the moon.

Alongside a woman to die for.

Congratulations, pal, you've just hit rock bottom.

Laughter and loud music filled the

darkness ahead. It came from the Pink Palace, silhouetted against the trees atop the bluff ahead. It was the sound of the rich enjoying themselves and it hit Mitch like a hard slap in the face.

It put him on red alert and he knew he'd have to stay that way if he was to survive the rest of the evening.

31

After years of lying dormant, the Pink Palace had finally come alive (resurrected, Elaina called it), flooding the Malibu night with all the drama and bursting brilliance of a neglected nova. Lights brightened every downstairs room and the huge kitchen bustled with caterers from Beverly Hills preparing caviar, bite-size hors d'oeuvres and popping open magnums of Cristal champagne. Outside, the black-tie engagement party was going full-tilt. A hundred or so guests, rounded up at the last moment by Claire and her secretary and whisked here in chauffeured limousines, were drinking and dancing to live music on the brightly lit terrace. Underwater lights glowed greenly in the swimming pool. Only the cabana was dark. But since no one was swimming, nobody (as Mitch had reasoned) noticed.

White-jacketed waiters moved among

the elegant bejeweled guests, making sure they had whatever they wanted; while Taggert, Mace and a squad of rent-a-cops, all wearing tuxes and ear-mikes, kept watch unobtrusively from the sidelines.

Claire and Edgar Bennett were among the couples slow-dancing on the terrace. She, wowing them in a little blue original from Paris and with half of Tiffany sparkling in her upswept golden hair; and he, no slouch in an elegant Pierre Cardin tuxedo that fitted like a cat burglar's glove.

Fred and Ginger never moved more gracefully or looked more romantic. To all appearances, a match made in heaven but in reality spawned in hell.

Edgar Bennett, as he and Claire swayed to the music, whispered in her ear: 'What a wonderful idea this was.'

'I'm glad you're enjoying yourself.'

'Were you worried I wouldn't?'

'Well, you're not exactly the playboy of the modern world.'

For a moment, he stopped wondering about Claire's real intentions and gave a rare smile. 'That'll be news to all my jet-set friends.'

'A sense of humor?' Claire arched her eyebrows in mock surprise. 'Edgar, I'm seeing a whole new side to you tonight.' They danced on, returning the nods and smiles of other couples dancing around them.

Upstairs, sitting in the dark at her bedroom window, Elaina watched her sister and stepfather dancing in bemused wonderment, thinking: *Wouldn't all you lovely people like to know what's going on inside their conniving little brains. Why, most of you'd pay more than your alimony payments to get the real lowdown. Even in La-La Land, a place famous for its liberal lifestyles, a stepfather murdering his wife so he could marry his stepdaughter was bizarre enough to start the bistro set gossiping. They would raise their eyebrows and speculate about propriety and long-lost American morals; while some of the old guard, fighting to rise above the ever-burgeoning mainstream of youth, might come right out and say it was wrong.*

Most of the young Turks wouldn't agree with them, but as a group they would have killed to know exactly what was behind it all. And Elaina, if she had known, would have gladly told them. Shouted it from the rooftops, in fact. But she didn't; she was just as much in the dark as everyone else. And with all the secrecy going on around her, it didn't look like she'd know any time in the near future. God, she was lucky to even be there . . .

Earlier that day, in San Marino, Edgar had said flatly that she wasn't coming. This was his evening, his and her sister's, and he wasn't going to have Elaina spoil it with one of her drunken tantrums. Great, Elaina retorted. That was fine with her. She didn't want to go anyway. She'd only have to spend the evening trying to field all the slyly couched questions thrown her way about how she felt about her own sister marrying their stepfather, for God's sake.

But for reasons Elaina couldn't fathom, Claire wanted her there. She insisted upon it in fact, even though she knew it was pissing Edgar off. Tell you what, she told him. How about if Elaina drinks nothing stronger than ginger ale, can she come then? Fat chance, Edgar snorted. That'll last what, all of ten seconds? Screw him, Elaina said when Claire brought her the news. You want me to lay off the booze, you got it. And no coke, either, Claire added. My nose is sealed, Elaina said. She giggled and sucked her thumb. For you, sister mine, I'll even give up having sex in public. *That* most of all, Claire said. And that's how it was settled.

Now, as she watched everyone partying below, Elaina knew it was not drinking or drugs she had to fear but the lust fermenting in her brain and between her thighs. It burned out of control. She fought it for as long as she could; then, finally overwhelmed by her sexual desires, she put her thumb in her mouth and gently started sucking. It helped, like a quick fix, but it wasn't a cure-all. That she could only find downstairs. Suddenly she thought: My God, I'm like Dracula. As long as I keep getting laid, I'll live forever!

Someone was giggling in the darkness. She realized with horror that it was her. Something in her brain snapped, regressed, and she heard her father's twangy drawling voice say: 'Well, if you can't fight 'em, little gal, join 'em.'

'I think I will, daddy,' she told him. Still sucking her thumb, she looked out the window at the partygoers below, searching for her next victim. It took a few moments before she spotted him, but the instant she did she knew he was it, the one man Claire and Edgar would hate her to seduce most, a man they'd already chased out of society.

How fitting, she thought. How Jesus Christ of me. I think I'll go down there and save him, poor devil.

32

Mitch toiled up the steep path that climbed curving to the bluff. Thanks to Donna's Lifecycle, which he rode whenever he had the time, he reached the top without feeling winded.

Ahead, all he could see was the bougainvillea purpling the property walls. He paused, listening to make sure he was alone. The only sounds were the wind off the ocean and the general uproar of the party. Satisfied, Mitch followed the path, now level and paved with flagstone, to an iron gate hanging between two pillars atop which sat two stone falcons. Mitch did not know it but real estate myth claimed the birds were a gift to the original owner from the immortal Rudolph Valentino, the two being lovers, some said, when the silent film star lived at Falcon Lair. But that was a crock: the Pink Palace had not even been built by 1926, when tormented Rudy took his final bow in New York. In actual fact the twin stone falcons were nothing but an afterthought, put there by a greedy landscaper trying to gouge every last cent out of the absentee billionaire owner.

Mitch checked his watch. The luminous dial showed 9:51. He was slightly ahead of schedule. He tried the gate. It was open. Silently thanking Claire for remembering to unlock it, he followed the path through a jungle of foliage to a white gazebo, its latticework overgrown with rambling roses.

Mitch peered around the side of the gazebo at the cabana. Fifty feet of flood-lighted lawn separated the two structures. He knew, as he'd known when he'd seen it in the daylight, that it was pure suicide to try to cross the grass without being seen. He checked his watch again: 9:56. Four minutes to wait. He reached for his Camels, remembering as he did that he had deliberately left them in the car in case he'd gotten the urge to smoke. In today's almost smokeless culture, the smell would have given him away. He knew he had been smart, but that did not lessen the urge. Mitch slipped a piece of chewing gum in his mouth and leaned back against a giant banana palm, thinking: *Okay, baby, now it's up to you.*

★   ★   ★

'Baby' was still dancing with the man she hated enough to murder. She sneaked a look at her watch. Nestled among sapphires and diamonds, the tiny hands showed the time to be seconds from ten o'clock. Christ, she was going to be late!

'What's wrong?' Edgar Bennett asked her as she stopped dancing.

'I think my heel's coming off,' Claire said. 'Excuse me a minute while I go change shoes.' Leaving him at the edge of the dance floor, she hurried across the terrace and up the steps to the villa. At the door she paused, as if to remove her shoe, at the same time looking back at Edgar. He was turned away from her, talking to some guests. Claire ran around the side of the villa, following a dirt path that led to the circuit-breaker box.

Opening the box, she turned off the switch marked 'Terrace-Pool area.' Everything outside went dark. Startled gasps came from the guests. They stood still, frozen in whatever position the darkness had caught them, anxiously looking around.

Someone shouted: 'Hey, Edgar, did you forget to pay your electric bill?'

Everyone laughed.

'What's the matter with you people?' Edgar Bennett joked. 'Haven't you heard of 'Dancing in the Dark'?' He hummed the old classic and everyone laughed and went on talking.

Taggert and Mace joined Edgar Bennett. 'It must be an overload,' he told them. 'Check the box.' They hurried off.

In the dark beside the villa Claire stood by the circuit-breaker box, anxiously counting off the thirty seconds Mitch had said he needed to reach the cabana without being seen.

★ ★ ★

While the lights were still out, Mitch ran to the side door of the cabana. As he went

268

to open the door, it suddenly opened and a tall dark figure stepped out. Startled, Mitch flattened himself against the wall. The figure, Braithwaite, made sure his zipper was closed and hurried back to the party.

So, Mitch thought, the good doctor makes more than house calls. That meant there was a woman still in the cabana. Mitch sweated it out hoping that whoever was inside would leave before his thirty seconds was up. But no one came out. And with time almost up, he was forced to duck inside. Three seconds later, right on schedule, the outside lights came back on amid rousing cheers. Good girl, Mitch thought, and closed the door.

It was dark in the cabana save for a bar of outside light coming in through a broken louvered blind. Mitch looked about him. He saw nothing unusual, but as he started to relax, a sound in the corner made him grab for his gun. He inched forward and saw a dim figure watching him from a chaise-lounge cushion lying on the floor.

'Judas,' he said softly. 'I should've

'known it'd be you.'

'Silly me,' Elaina said. She giggled and drank from a half-empty bottle of vodka. 'I got dressed too soon.'

'There's always tomorrow,' he said, hoping she wouldn't cause a scene.

'If you think that,' Elaina said, 'you have egg nog for brains.'

'I thought you said I was cute?'

'You are, real cute, but before you worry about humoring me, ask yourself this, Holden — are you ready to die on a cross and get up the next morning, still wanting to save the world even though it's full of people whose only goal in life is to steal, cheat, lie, and exterminate themselves?'

'Not me,' said Mitch. 'I leave that up to the guys with white collars.'

'Because if you aren't,' she went on, 'and I very much doubt if you are, get off your high horse and get down here in the mud with me and see how the rest of us suffer. You think I'm kidding?' she said as he just stared at her. 'Well, kid about this,' she opened her legs and prepared to rape herself with the bottle.

Mitch lunged forward, grabbed the bottle and wrenched it away from her, 'Crazy little . . .' He threw it behind the lounge chairs stacked beside her.

'Well, well, well,' she said. 'So we do care about me after all?'

'Shut up,' he said, furious. 'You think you got a corner on caring? You don't. Lots of people care, about lots of things. Only you're too busy scraping the bottom of the barrel to notice.'

'You mean, Seymour?' She shrugged. 'He's okay — for a slime-ball.' She giggled around her thumb. 'He's just what the doctor ordered, in fact.'

'Cute.'

'Just trying to save the world.'

'Trying to drive your sister crazy, you mean.'

'She told you about Braithwaite?' Elaina took her thumb from her mouth in surprise. 'Wow.'

'No big deal. Everybody gets dumped.'

'Not my sister. Dump her, buddy boy, and she'll see you get screwed ten ways to Christmas.'

'You got it all wrong: she dumped him.'

'It's *you* who's got it all wrong. I was there, remember? I even tried to warn him about her. But the big famous doctor thought he was too smart to listen to me, Little Miss Marshmallow Brain. Next thing he knew one of those tabloid photographers was snapping pictures through a motel window, getting blowups of him playing slap'n tickle with two teenage hookers Claire paid to come on to him at the club.'

'Keep going.'

'That's it. The next day the photos hit the newsstands and Dr. San Marino's life was over. No hospital would touch him, patients he'd had for years acted like he had AIDS and his wife of twenty-five years took him to the cleaners. All he had left was life in a bottle and Braithwaite took to it like a kid to candy.'

'He didn't look like a drunk to me.'

'He isn't. Not now. Thanks to Claire, who had Edgar put him on a lifetime retainer, he's a member of F.R.A — fraternity of recovering alcoholics. But his balls belong to her and that's just the way she wants it.' She broke off suddenly, as if struck by a clear and brilliant thought, and said with childlike innocence: 'Did you read *Catcher in the Rye*, like I asked?'

'Not yet. First, I'd like you to do something for me.'

'What?'

He helped her up, took out his wallet and showed her the piece of jigsaw puzzle. 'Lionel gave me this. Said he wanted you to have it.'

'Why?'

'Turn it over.'

She did. Mitch dug out his lighter, thumbed the wheel and a flame flared. He pointed to the back of the piece of jigsaw puzzle.

'See what's written there?'

'I-LOVE-YOU.' She giggled and sucked her thumb. 'That's cute.'

'What's it mean to you?'

'You love me?'

'What else?'

'Nothing, unless you're proposing.'

'Sure?'

She nodded. 'I've never even seen it before.'

"Course you haven't,' he said, suddenly realizing where he had gone wrong. 'Now I'm the one being stupid.' He tucked the lighter and piece of jigsaw puzzle in his pocket. Looked at his watch. It was almost time. 'You gotta get out of here, princess.'

'Why? Nobody will miss us. They're all too busy celebrating my sister's *coup*.'

'That's an odd way of putting it.'

'I'm an odd little girl, haven't you heard?' She tried to pull him down onto the chaise lounge cushion. When he resisted, she said: 'C'mon, Holden, this is your last chance to do me.'

'Go in the house and wait for me. I'll be along soon.'

'No. Stay here or I'll scream.'

He clipped her on the chin. 'Sorry,' he said as she fell into his arms. 'You gave me no choice.' He looked around, wondering where he could hide her. It was then he noticed that the rubber rafts stacked beside the chaise lounges weren't as neatly piled as he remembered.

Supporting Elaina with one arm, he dug out his lighter, thumbed it alight and

274

held the flame close to the top raft. The flame showed fingerprints in the thick white dust covering it; there was also a slight bulge as if something was hidden under it. Mitch lifted the top raft and saw the nickel-plated .32 pistol lying there.

'Hel-lo . . . '

He carried Elaina to the linen closet, gently put her inside, dumped her crutches in after her and closed the door. He then returned to the rubber rafts, picked up the gun, emptied out the bullets, and put the gun back where he found it. As he was covering it with the top rubber raft, he heard voices outside. He went to the window, peered through a crack in the blind and saw Claire and Edgar Bennett approaching, arm-in-arm.

'What kind of surprise?' Edgar was asking.

'If I tell you, darling, it won't be a surprise. Now, come on. Humor me.'

Mitch flattened himself against the wall by the door. Claire expected him to be there and it was her job to keep Edgar Bennett from seeing him. Mitch screwed a silencer onto his gun and waited.

The door opened and Claire led Edgar Bennett in.

'We mustn't be long,' he said. 'Our guests will wonder where we are.'

'Let them. This is our night, not theirs.' She turned and faced Mitch, a shadow she could barely see, adding: 'Or should I say 'our' night?'

Edgar Bennett turned and saw Mitch step forward, gun aimed at him.

'W-What the hell — ?'

'Aptly put, Edgar,' Claire said. 'It's exactly where you're going.' Then, to Mitch: 'Do it. What're you waiting for?' she said when Mitch didn't shoot. 'Kill him!'

'First, I want to ask him something.' Mitch turned to Edgar Bennett. 'On the day your wife was killed, you were supposed to be in the boat, right?'

'What business is that of yours?' Edgar Bennett snapped. 'Who are you?'

'But at the last minute,' Mitch pressed on, 'you got a call from Sheriff Briggs and didn't go.'

'How'd you know that?' Edgar Bennett turned to Claire. 'If this is some kind of joke — '

'No joke,' she said. Then to Mitch: 'Shoot the bastard, will you?'

'All in good time . . . ' He wagged the gun at Edgar Bennett. 'Tell me what Briggs wanted.'

Edgar Bennett didn't answer. Mitch cocked back the hammer.

'I can do like she wants, shoot you.'

Edgar Bennett said angrily: 'The sheriff told me the animal rights people were up in arms about my proposed ski resort and were on their way to picket my house. Said I was to stay inside, no matter what, and not do anything until he arrived.'

'He's lying,' Claire broke in. 'There wasn't any phone call. He bribed Briggs to say he called him, so he'd have an alibi for not going out in the boat.'

'No,' Mitch said patiently, 'the call was legit. I had the sheriff FAX me a copy of the phone company records, along with his sworn statement he gave the D.A.'

While Mitch was talking, Claire inched toward the pile of rubber rafts.

'What're you trying to say — that Edgar didn't blow up the boat?'

'How could he, when you and Lionel

rigged the whole thing.'

'Lionel?' Edgar Bennett said, surprised. 'Our former chauffeur?'

'Don't listen to him,' Claire exclaimed. 'He's crazy. If anybody did any rigging,' she added to Mitch, 'it was Elaina, not me. She loved him, remember?'

'Wrong. You loved him, she just banged him.' He tucked the gun away, took the piece of jigsaw puzzle from his pocket and showed it to Claire. 'For a long time I thought Elaina wrote what's on the back, but she didn't. You did.'

'I don't know what you're talking about.' Claire slowly reached back behind her, under the top rubber raft, and felt for the gun she had hidden there earlier.

'A handwriting expert will prove I'm right. All he has to do is compare it to the note you left me in the cottage at Lake Tahoe — '

'You two were in Tahoe together?' Edgar Bennett said, shocked.

'Diddling our brains out,' Mitch said. 'Sorry.'

'You're going to be a lot more than sorry.' Claire pulled the gun from under the top raft and aimed it at Mitch. 'You fucking moron. You just signed your own death warrant.'

'I signed that long ago, baby, the moment I hooked up with you.' Mitch turned to Edgar Bennett. 'The plan was for me to shoot you and then run out the back before anyone saw me. Claire would give the cops a phony description of the shooter and then we'd ride off into the sunset together.' He paused, letting his words sink in, then said to Claire: 'Only you had another agenda: you planned to shoot me before I left here and claim self-defense.'

'Is that true?' Edgar Bennett asked Claire.

'Shut up!' She turned to Mitch. 'Give me your gun.'

Mitch took his gun out of his pants and handed it to Claire. She swapped it for her gun and aimed Mitch's .45 at Edgar Bennett.

'Goodbye, darling . . . '

'Claire, no — ' The words froze on his lips as she coldly pulled the trigger. CLICK. Then again. CLICK. And again.

CLICK. Infuriated, she dropped the .45 and aimed her own gun at him, pulling the trigger, CLICK, CLICK, CLICK!

For an instant she looked stunned. Then it dawned on her. 'Bastard!' she said to Mitch. 'You sold me out!'

'How 'bout that?'

'B-But, why?'

'Just playin' a hunch.' Taking the .38 from her, he picked up his own gun and tucked both weapons into his pockets.

Claire mentally heard the harsh clang of prison bars closing. She reached out and clutched Mitch's hand with both of hers, pleading:

'Please, can't we work this out?'

Mitch looked at her, stunned by her gall.

'I got greedy, darling. I made a mistake.'

Edgar Bennett shook his head in disbelief. 'You call killing your mother and maiming your sister a — *mistake?*'

Claire ignored him. Her only salvation lay in Mitch and she knew, from experience, he was easy pickings.

'At the cottage we had something special . . . you said so, yourself.'

'I was wrong. That was lust talking.'

'Don't you mean love?'

'No. For me, one has nothin' to do with the other.'

'You mean you never loved me?'

'I'd be a liar if I said that.'

'Then nothing's changed.'

'Everything's changed,' Mitch said, 'Whatever I once felt for you is now gone.'

'Yet you continued to act like we were partners? Why?'

'I felt like I owed it to myself to wipe the slate clean.' When he saw she did not understand him, he said: 'I needed to clear my conscience, no matter what the consequences.'

'You devious, self-serving dirt-bag!'

'Hey, I warned you when we first met that maybe I wasn't as corrupt as I pretended. Remember?'

Claire studied Mitch and saw no forgiveness in his yellow-gray eyes.

'I misjudged you, Holliday.'

'Most people do. But, just to show you what a forgiving guy I am, we'll let Edgar, here, decide what to do with you.' Mitch grinned at Edgar Bennett. 'Your call, pal.'

'Edgar, please . . . ' Claire turned those

incredible pale blue eyes on him.

'Forget it,' he told her. 'You're going away for a long, long time.'

'I wouldn't count on that, sister mine . . .'

Startled, they whirled around.

Elaina stood in the linen closet doorway, supported by her crutches. She held a small automatic in one hand and rubbed her jaw with the other.

'Elaina, sweetie . . . ' Claire said, as if reprieved.

Elaina ignored her and looked at Mitch. 'That's the second time you've slugged me, Holden.'

'Sorry, princess.'

'It's all right. I'm glad you did. You hadn't, I would've missed the whole second act.'

'Sweetie, the gun — give me the gun.' Claire started toward Elaina, who leveled the gun at her sister's chest, warning: 'Don't come any closer.'

'Elaina, I can explain everything.'

'You don't have to. I've already heard everything.' She indicated the closet. 'And I didn't like any of it.'

'Put the gun down,' Mitch told her. 'It's over.'

'It'll be over when she's dead,' Elaina said, 'like momma.' She turned to Claire. 'You're the one who caused the boat to explode — '

'Elaina, please, I can explain — '

'You killed momma and took away my legs. And all this time I thought it was you, Popsy . . . ' She turned to Edgar Bennett: 'That's why I brought the gun, so I could shoot you tonight and end this nightmare, once and for all.' She looked back at Claire. 'Well, now it's ended.'

'No, don't, please — ' Claire backed away, hands held before her as if trying to ward off the bullets.

'Princess — ' Mitch started for Elaina. But before he could reach her, she fired twice, both bullets hitting Claire in the chest. She staggered back against Edgar Bennett, almost knocking him down, and collapsed on the floor. Dead.

Elaina then quickly put the barrel of the gun in her mouth — 'Bye bye, Holden' — and pulled the trigger.

Blood and bits of flesh and skull spattered on the wall behind her.

Mitch lunged and caught her falling

body in his arms. He gently lowered her to the floor. She smiled up at him, fading fast.

'Y-You're . . . cute . . . '

She tried to put her left thumb in her mouth but died before she could get it there.

Mitch held her thumb for several moments, feeling his guts in turmoil, then released all his pent-up emotions in a long, heavy sigh.

He then gently folded Elaina's hands across her breast. That was when he noticed it on the palms of her white cotton gloves.

'Christ.'

'What?' said Edgar Bennett.

Mitch ignored him. He peeled Elaina's gloves back. He did not want to believe what he saw but there was no denying it: there, in the middle of each palm, blood was seeping from a small ragged hole.

'My God,' Edgar Bennett said. 'How'd she get those?'

'We'll never know,' Mitch said and as he said it, he felt cold all over.

284

33

The Santa Anas were gone and the sun was back to smiling through the smog again — a pale brown haze that lay trapped above the Valley by the surrounding mountains. No one liked the smog, any more than they liked the earthquakes, floods, fires or the winds stirring up their allergies. But it was all part of the package known as Los Angeles and the good news was, the smog was actually lessening.

'According to statistics,' Mitch was quick to say when some out-of-towner grumbled about the smog, 'it's thirty percent better now than back in the '50s. And gettin' less all the time.'

But today his mind was not on smog. As he fondly polished the now-repaired orange-and-white Oldsmobile Starfire in the shade of the walnut trees, he kept glancing toward the street, looking for the mailman, hoping that today would be the day when a letter finally arrived from the D.A.'s office notifying him that his private investigator's license had been renewed.

He had Edgar Bennett to thank for that. Deciding that he did not need any more adverse publicity, the billionaire had blamed Elaina's unbalanced state of mind for Claire's shooting, calling the whole thing a ghastly tragic accident that would haunt him for the rest of his life. He also explained away the holes in her palms by saying Elaina had deliberately stabbed herself in an effort to get attention. Because of his money and power, and his influence over the District Attorney, no one pressed him for any other explanation. Nor did he make any attempt to drag Mitch into the sordid drama. He told the detectives who arrived on the scene less than ten minutes after Edgar Bennett notified the District Attorney, that Mr. Holliday was an old friend of the family and should be treated with the same 'respect, care, and understanding' that he, himself, expected at this, his greatest moment of grief.

Mitch was grateful for Edgar Bennett's support, but suspicious of his motive:

after all, he had plotted with Claire to kill the man, and though he had not gone through with it and in fact had saved Edgar's life, it was still something that Mitch, in Edgar's shoes, would not have overlooked as quickly or graciously. But Edgar Bennett genuinely seemed to like Mitch. He invited him over to the house and to the country club and even offered him a position as head of security for BENCO's three California-based subsidiary companies. Mitch thanked him for the generous offer and agreed to think about it, which he did (for all of five seconds), and then politely turned him down. Edgar Bennett took the rejection better than Mitch expected, knowing the billionaire's penchant for power trips, and after the two shook hands he asked Mitch if there was anything he could do for him.

'Well,' Mitch said, not wanting to build up his hopes, 'I do have this problem in gettin' my P.I. license renewed . . .'

Now, as Mitch rubbed the final smear of polish from the gleaming white hood of the Olds, Richie and Marjean came running out of the house, soccer ball in hand, screaming for Mitch to play with them.

'He can't,' Donna called out from the front yard. 'His Lordship is too busy shining that pile of junk he calls a classic.' She was digging at him he knew, because earlier she had asked him to help her keep an eye on the garage sale items arranged on the sidewalk grass and he'd refused.

'You heard your mom,' Mitch told them. 'I'm all tied up. But,' he added, slipping them a wink, 'as Lord of Reseda it's my duty to make all my subjects happy. And after I've washed up, I'll be taking anyone who wants to go for a drive in the most beautiful chariot Detroit ever made. What?' he said as they didn't respond. 'You don't believe me?'

Eyes accusing saucers, lips tightly compressed, they slowly shook their heads.

'Urgh!' Mitch pretended to stab himself in the heart. 'I'm hurt. I'm really hurt.' He collapsed dramatically on the ground.

Giggling, Marjean grabbed the soccer ball from her brother and bounced it off of Mitch's chest. He gasped, sat up, and grabbed for her. But she eluded his grasp, and screaming with laughter ran over and kicked the ball to Richie. He trapped it deftly and began dribbling the ball around his sister.

Mitch got up, brushed the dirt from his T-shirt and shorts and joined Donna on the sidewalk.

'Did you hear those guys? They didn't believe me.'

'Why should they? You're always promising to take us for a ride in that chrome monster and then wimping out at the last minute.'

'I do not,' Mitch protested. 'I have never wimped out on anyone in my entire life — ' He broke off as behind them, Richie kicked the football and it landed among some used books that Donna had piled on a wobbly old table. The table collapsed, books spilling everywhere.

'I told you not to kick the ball this way,' she scolded her son. 'Now look what you've done.'

'Calm down, nothing's broken — ' Mitch paused as he noticed something on the ground at his feet. It was an open book with a thin silver key taped to the inside of the cover. Picking it up, he turned it over and saw it was John O'Hara's *Appointment in Samarra*. The old dog-eared cover jogged his memory and suddenly he remembered Lionel buying it one lunchtime when they were tailing a suspect who was shopping in the Northridge Mall.

'What've you got?' Donna asked, peering over his shoulder.

'A key.' He showed her the open book. 'It was taped in here.'

'That's odd. Lionel never told me he had a safe deposit — ' She broke off and locked gazes with Mitch as both suddenly got the same idea. 'My God,' she said in a hushed voice. 'You don't think . . . ?'

'Only one way to find out,' Mitch said. 'Give me a moment to change clothes and we'll go down to the bank and see what Lionel was up to.'

★ ★ ★

They drove to the bank on Ventura Boulevard, the bank in which Donna had her checking account, and, sure enough, Lionel had a safe deposit box there. The bank official was reluctant at first to let them examine the box. But when Mitch called over the acting assistant manager, explained Lionel was dead and showed her the death certificate he had had Sheriff Briggs track down and send to Donna, the woman gave Donna the okay.

Once in the vault, the bank official laid the flat metal box on a table in front of Mitch and Donna and left them alone. For a moment they both stared at the box, unable to make themselves open it. Then, 'You do it,' she told him. 'I'm shaking so bad, I might drop the damn thing.'

Mitch wet his lips and opened it, lifting the lid with the same heart-stopping expectation that burns inside an archeologist opening a Pharaoh's tomb for the first time. Inside, the box was filled with a pile of glittering jewelry.

For one fleeting moment the two of them stared at the diamond rings, bracelets, pendants, and earrings in silent disbelief. Then:

'Oh-my-God,' Donna whispered.

'Elaina's missing jewelry,' Mitch said, equally awed. 'All one million bucks of it.'

They stood there in silence, eyes riveted on the jewelry.

'Well,' Mitch said finally, 'I guess all your financial worries are over. You and the kids will be set for life for what we get for these.'

'What're you saying? We can't keep 'em.'

'Are you nuts?'

'But, they're not ours.'

'Finders keepers — '

'Don't be ridiculous. You find twenty bucks in the street, maybe. Not a million dollars' worth of somebody else's jewels.'

'But that 'somebody else' is dead, remember. And so's her sister.'

'Doesn't matter. There must be other relatives.'

'Only one I know of — a stepfather named Edgar Bennett who just happens to already have all the money in the world!'

'I don't care. This jewelry is stolen and I won't have my kids benefiting from — '

Mitch stopped her, 'Hey, change gears, will you? Aren't you forgettin' your husband? Lionel paid for these with his life — that's got to count for somethin'.'

'Nice try, Mr. Holliday, but I'm not buying. Lionel checked out because of a blown tire. You said so yourself.'

'I don't give a damn what I said. The jewelry's rightfully yours,' Mitch said firmly. 'You were married to a jerk who never did anythin' for you or the kids, a guy who only looked out for himself till the day he died, and now, through a stroke of Fate — 'cause that's what the blowout was — has managed to make you and the kids' futures suddenly look a whole lot brighter. It's like the story of — '

'Mitch, the last thing I need right now is one of your shade tree parables.

'Anyway,' Mitch continued, ignoring her blast, 'the truth is Lionel wanted you to have these. He told me so.'

'Baloney.'

'I kid you not. When Lionel was dyin', he told me the key was in the book. I just didn't understand what he was sayin' then. But now, hey, it all makes sense. And you'd be a damn fool if you don't take what Fate's offering.'

'Then I'm a damn fool,' Donna said stubbornly. 'Now, you gonna call Mr. Bennett or am I?'

Mitch looked at her a moment then suddenly grinned.

'What's so funny?'

'You,' he said. 'You're really somethin'.'

'Shut up and make the call.'

'I already have.'

'What d'you mean?' she said. 'When?'

'Earlier. Back at the boat. Right after I changed clothes. One of Bennett's company choppers is picking us up at Van Nuys airport in exactly' — he checked his watch — 'twelve minutes.'

Donna looked confused. 'I don't get it. If you'd already talked to Bennett, why a minute ago were you trying to make me take — ?' She stopped as it hit her, then, 'Damn you!' she exploded. 'You were testing me, you bastard! Seeing if I'd — '

Mitch grabbed her in a bear hug, and kissed her.

'Oh, no you don't,' she said, pushing

him away. 'No way you're gonna smooth talk your way out of this.' But she let him kiss her again, anyway. And this time when they broke apart, she did not say anything but looked up into his battered smiling face and saw something in his yellow-gray eyes she had never seen before: genuine affection for her.

'We have to get out of here,' he said gently. 'Otherwise, Bennett's guys are gonna think we're not comin'.'

34

Ten minutes later one of BENCO Industries' company choppers picked Mitch and Donna up at Van Nuys airport and flew them across town to LAX, where Edgar Bennett's corporate jet was preparing to fly him to New York for a board meeting.

An efficient-looking secretary was waiting for them as they climbed out of the helicopter, and after hastily introducing herself as 'Ms. Reed,' she rushed them across the windy tarmac and on board the sleek blue-and-white Gulfstream G200.

'Please be seated,' she told them. 'I'll notify the boss you're here.' She hurried to the rear of the plane where a group of young executives sat at a small conference table, cluttered with files and laptops, discussing business. Squeezing past them, she disappeared through a doorway.

'I'm sure glad we're giving him back his jewelry,' Mitch grinned as he and Donna sank into the soft buttery-leather seats. 'As you can see, poor old Edgar's a real hardship case.'

'Shut up,' Donna said. 'Only thing I want to hear out of you is why?'

'Why, what?'

'Why you called Bennett *before* you actually knew the jewels were in the safe deposit box. I mean, you couldn't have known 'cause you didn't even know Lionel had a box.'

'I didn't know and yet I did know,' Mitch said. 'After Lionel told me to find 'a key', you know, when he was dyin', I kept trying to figure out what he meant and, well, a safe deposit box was the only thing that made any sense.' He chuckled, amused by a thought, said: 'Guess I'm not such a Saint Simple Simon, after all.'

'Who?' Donna looked at him, confused. 'What're you talking about?'

Before Mitch could reply, Edgar Bennett's secretary returned and escorted them back to his office. It was tiny but luxuriously appointed, the walls adorned with photos of Edgar Bennett shaking hands with just about every important executive and political leader in the modern world.

As the secretary ushered Mitch and Donna in, Edgar Bennett looked up from the international stock-market figures he had been studying on his computer and gave Mitch a wolfish smile.

'Welcome to the lion's den, Holliday. Change your mind about my offer?'

Mitch shook his head and introduced Donna to Edgar Bennett, who rose and shook her hand.

'Whatever it is you want to tell me,' he told them crisply, 'make it quick. We're heading for the Friendly Skies in five minutes.'

'Don't look at me,' Mitch said. 'This is all her show.'

'Mr. Bennett,' Donna said nervously, 'I have something that belongs to you.' She opened her purse, took out a clear plastic 'Baggie' filled with the stolen jewelry and set it on the desk before Edgar Bennet.

His eyebrows arched in surprise. 'W-Where'd you get these?'

'Elaina gave them to my husband to keep,' Donna said. 'I've no idea why, but they were in his safe deposit box and when Mitch, here, told me who they originally belonged to, I thought we should turn them over to you.'

Edgar Bennett looked at Donna, his expression a mixture of surprise and amazement.

'That was very . . . uhm . . . generous of you, Mrs. Banks.' He looked at Mitch with a slightly taunting smile. 'Both of you.'

'That's us,' Mitch said cheerfully. 'The Generosity Twins.'

Donna glared witheringly at Mitch and then told Edgar Bennett: 'We'll be leaving now.'

'No, wait,' he said. 'We're not through here yet.' He looked at Mitch. 'When you turned down the job as head of my security, did you know about this jewelry?'

'No.'

'I'm glad. I might need your services one day and it's reassuring to know that one of us has integrity.'

'I'll remind you of that when the day comes,' Mitch said.

'I'm sure you will.' Edgar Bennett came around his desk, rested his hands on Donna's shoulders and looked into her big dark eyes. 'You're a remarkable woman, Mrs. Banks. Maybe the most remarkable woman I've ever had the pleasure of meeting.'

'Why? Because I'm honest — or stupid?'

Edgar Bennett didn't answer. After looking into her eyes for another moment, he turned and punched the speakerphone on his desk. 'Call the tower, Randy, and let them know we won't be taking off for a few more minutes.'

'Yessir.'

Edgar Bennett punched another button. 'Come in here, will you, Toby?' He smiled at Donna. 'Now that we have a moment, may I offer you something to drink?'

'No, thanks.'

'What's the problem?' Mitch asked.

'No problem,' Edgar Bennett said. He paused as a short, plump, balding man in a gray suit entered carrying a corporate checkbook, and stood before him. 'Yes, Mr. Bennett?'

'Toby, write Mrs. Banks a check for

one hundred thousand dollars, will you?'

Donna gaped. 'Mr. Bennett, you don't have to — '

'Pay you the reward? Why not?'

'You were offering a reward?'

'Damn right.' Edgar Bennett looked at Mitch without blinking. 'Ten percent of the jewelry's estimated value. Isn't that right, Toby?'

'Y-Yes, sir.' The accountant gulped down the lie, opened the checkbook, took out a pen and forced himself to smile at Donna. 'Would you mind spelling out your full name, Mrs. Banks?'

★   ★   ★

A few minutes later, as Mitch and Donna were crossing the tarmac toward the awaiting chopper, its whirling rotors tugging at their hair and blowing dust into their squinted eyes, she suddenly grabbed his arm.

'Let's all go out to dinner tonight, you know, and splurge; wanna?'

All he could hear was the roar of the rotors. 'What?'

She repeated herself, shouting so he could hear her.

'Great idea,' Mitch yelled. 'I'll even break down and drive the Olds.'

'Ho. Ho. Ho.'

'This time I mean it! I swear, on my mother's grave, I'll drive the Olds.'

'My God,' Donna said. 'I believe you're actually serious. Wonders never cease.' Laughing, she reached up and kissed him. Then, hand-in-hand, they ran toward the awaiting chopper.

THE END

We do hope that you have enjoyed reading this large print book.

Did you know that all of our titles are available for purchase?

We publish a wide range of high quality large print books including:
Romances, Mysteries, Classics
General Fiction
Non Fiction and Westerns

Special interest titles available in large print are:
The Little Oxford Dictionary
Music Book, Song Book
Hymn Book, Service Book

Also available from us courtesy of Oxford University Press:
Young Readers' Dictionary
(large print edition)
Young Readers' Thesaurus
(large print edition)

For further information or a free brochure, please contact us at:
Ulverscroft Large Print Books Ltd.,
The Green, Bradgate Road, Anstey,
Leicester, LE7 7FU, England.
Tel: (00 44) **0116 236 4325**
Fax: (00 44) **0116 234 0205**

Other titles in the
Linford Mystery Library:

THE MISSING HEIRESS MURDERS

John Glasby

Private eye Johnny Merak's latest client, top Mob man Enrico Manzelli, has received death-threats. A menacing man himself, he pressures Johnny to discover who was sending them — and why. Then Barbara Minton, a rich heiress, disappears, and her husband turns to Johnny. Despite Manzelli's ultimatum — that Johnny should focus on his case alone — he takes the job. But that's before he discovers the fate of the first detective Minton hired. And more bodies are stacking up . . .